MW01620654

The Reunion

The Reunion

Jack Weyland

Deseret Book Company
Salt Lake City, Utah

Printed in the United States of America
First printing February 1982
Second printing October 1983

Library of Congress Cataloging in Publication Data

Weyland, Jack, 1940-
The reunion.

I. Title.
PS3573.E99R4 813'.54 81-19595
ISBN 0-87747-892-9 AACR2

To Sherry

Who can find a virtuous woman?
For her price is far above rubies.

She learneth to make whole wheat bread,
even though she's a convert from Queens, New York.

She stayeth up late at night,
doing visual aids for her Primary calling.

She hath studied music at BYU and singeth beautifully;
even though she liketh classical music,
yet she goeth with her husband to hear Kenny Rogers.

She keepeth romance in her marriage;
her husband is still madly in love with her.

She rescueth her husband from jaws of boredom
and duty and a never-ending "Things to Do" list.

When she is angry, she letteth her husband know,
and they talk it out, and then things get better.

When her husband writes, she alloweth him the luxury
of sitting for hours in front of a blank piece of paper,
without telling him that he should get up and do something useful,
like mowing the lawn.

Many women have done virtuously,
but thou excelleth them all.

CHAPTER ONE

Eric quit work at noon on Friday, hoping to help Janice with the details of farming out their children to friends for the weekend in order to get an early start to his high school reunion. Later he realized it was hopeless to have thought about leaving so early. The last time he had been on time for anything involving his family was the day he got married.

As he stepped from the gleaming white van with the giant green thumb and LAWN DOCTOR painted on the sides, one of his neighbors, a widow, called to him to inspect the new crop of weeds in her yard. She had never subscribed to his service, but since she was a member of the ward and he was her bishop, he examined her lawn and applied some weed killer for her.

Half an hour later, hot and sweaty in the white uniform designed to look medical, he entered the house and found himself in the middle of an Indian uprising.

Janice's Cub Scout den was performing a war dance in his living room. He stopped to watch the spectacle of Janice, six months pregnant, enthusiastically leading the dance. She winked as she passed, followed closely in a line by eight boys wildly chanting and beating their homemade tom-toms. One of them was his son Brent, the studious one wearing glasses and with a long string of plastic yellow beads and cloth arrows decorating his blue uniform.

Eric loved to look at his wife. After fifteen years of married life, he had her features memorized. Her Southern European nose and high cheekbones gave her face a strong classic beauty, as if her profile might be found sculptured on some ancient Greek vase.

Her long brown hair bounced in rhythm to the dance. She often talked about getting it cut. There's a limit, she would say, to how old a woman can be and still wear her hair this way. Please, he'd ask, just a little while more.

He retreated to the kitchen for a snack but found only two slices of bread in the breadbox. He made a peanut butter and jelly sandwich, but after one bite, his four-year-old daughter Cathy came in. "You made that just for me, didn't you, Daddy?" she said optimistically before walking away with it.

He watched the sandwich depart for the TV room and considered reminding Cathy of the family rule about not eating there, but gave it up as too much trouble.

Opening the refrigerator, he found cottage cheese for his weight-conscious fourteen-year-old daughter Kim. Other than that, all he found was a bottle of canned beets.

She has the Scouts, he thought, so there must be refreshments in the house. They won't miss it if I have some. But first to find it.

First he tried the freezer compartment of the refrigerator, hoping to find ice cream. He noticed the dead carp his seven-year-old son Doug had caught a year ago. Nobody wanted to eat it, but because it was the boy's first catch, they couldn't throw it out either—and so it stayed. There wasn't much else in the freezer except for some unidentified packages wrapped in tinfoil.

He looked in every cupboard but found nothing.

Finally he gave up and had a dish of beets.

It was strange about the beets. Nobody else in the family liked them. They called it Daddy's project. He planted and weeded them, ate the green tops in midsummer, picked and canned them in August, and then single-handedly ate beets the rest of the year.

A few weeks ago he realized something—he didn't like beets either.

"Now if you'll all be quiet," Janice announced to the boys in the living room. "Alan, don't beat on the coffee table with your spoon. I know it sounds nice, but it makes little marks on the table."

He loved her voice. She was a singer with a clear soprano voice that reminded him of cold mountain streams. She sang for most of the weddings and funerals in the ward. But even more than her singing ability, he loved the optimism and concern for others her voice conveyed. He was sure some ward members called him just to hear her answer the phone. "Why, Brother Johnson," she'd bubble, "how nice of you to call. How are you doing today?"

"Now if you'll all be quiet," she announced to the Cub Scouts, "I'll go and get our treats."

She danced into the kitchen.

"I hope that wasn't a fertility dance," he said with a grin.

She smiled back. "Hello, dear—you're home early."

Opening a cupboard, she carefully removed the camouflaging layer of canned corn and removed a covered cake dish. He pushed away his dish of beets and gazed at a German chocolate cake.

"The cake looks good," he hinted.

"Someday I'll make one just for you."

"Just a small piece?"

"There's just enough for the boys. I'm not even having any."

Brent came into the kitchen. "Mom, what are we going to do about my gerbil? We can't leave it all alone without food."

"We'll talk about it later," she said, busily serving the cake onto paper plates. "Is Alan behaving in there?"

"He's banging on the mirror with a spoon."

"Go ask him to stop. I'll be in with our cake in just a minute."

Brent left.

Eric walked behind Janice and kissed her on the back of the neck.

"Eric, please," she said, faking displeasure, "I'm on official Cub Scout business now."

"I'm so crazy about a woman in uniform," he whispered in her ear.

She laughed. "I know better—you just want some cake. I'm sorry, but I didn't know you'd be home this early. I should've made two. But if you want a snack, there're still some beets in the refrigerator."

"I had some. You know, from the back you don't even look pregnant."

She placed the last piece on a paper plate. He blew lightly in her ear.

"You're certainly in a good mood today," she said, relaxing in his arms.

"Do you know how long it's been since we got away, just the two of us?"

"A long time."

"Two years," he said. "We're going to have fun together this weekend."

She turned to look at him.

"What's wrong?" he asked.

"Your tone of voice when you say how much fun it's going to be."

"So?"

"Eric, you've been awfully busy lately. I know this may come as a shock to you, but—I'm going to have a baby. In about twelve weeks."

"Yeah, so?"

"So I'm not the most alluring woman in the world right now—unless you like looking at stretch marks. I feel like such a cow lately."

"You're always beautiful to me."

As she started to pick up the tray, he kissed her. She set the tray down again to enjoy his closeness.

Just then Alan opened the door to the kitchen, saw them, and moaned, "Yuck! They're kissing!"

She pulled away, laughing. "Just wait till this gets out. Think of the scandal—the bishop still kisses his wife. 'Bye, dear."

She left him with only a knife covered with frosting.

His son Doug breezed in, picked up the knife, and in one giant lick, finished it off.

Eric returned to the kitchen table, looked sadly at the bottle of beets, and went downstairs to his office.

The office door had two railings on which he could slide either the LAWN DOCTOR or ORANGE JULIUS signs. He ran both businesses at home.

He sat down at his desk, brushed away the current list of people to phone, and pulled out his old high school annual. He read the first page: "Ranger High School—Home of the Fighting Bulldogs."

Ranger sat in the middle of Montana, near enough to oil fields to have a refinery, close enough to agriculture and ranching areas to boast a sugar beet factory and a stockyard. Although he hadn't been back for several years, he still remembered the interesting mix of smells that occurred whenever the wind changed directions. Twenty years ago the town had been nearly 60,000 in size; now it was close to 100,000, with three high schools.

The class of '61 had consisted of 507 students, up to that time the largest class ever to graduate from the school. The members of the class were part of the "baby boom" coming from the Second World War. They simultaneously provided the soldiers who ended up in Viet Nam and the college students who protested the war.

Twenty years, he thought. What have I done with it?

Not enough, he answered. It's the story of my life. I made the mistake of becoming over-qualified.

He opened a file drawer and pulled out his Ph.D. degree. He kept it hidden away.

In 1961, with the nation still in a frenzy over Russia's Sputnik, he started college. The nation had accepted President Kennedy's challenge for the U.S. to land a man on the moon by 1970. For anyone with mathematical skills, it was almost a patriotic duty to go into science. The nation needed him.

He attended college for a year, went on his mission, returned two years later, enrolled again, met Janice shortly after, got married, then spent the next seven years—through a B.S. degree, then onto graduate school —in crackerjack apartments, sending his wife to coin-operated laundromats with diapers three times a week, dreaming for the day when he would be Doctor Turner, when the job offers would roll in like the tide. He finished in 1971, the year the bottom dropped from the Ph.D. job market, when scientists with twenty publications ended up driving cabs.

He had done what many others did, which was to hope that things would improve, that it was only temporary. In the meantime there were always post-doctorate research appointments. He worked an extra two years with his thesis adviser, continuing the same research he had done for his Ph.D.; he received just enough money for that to scrape by.

That ended, and he found a one-year teaching appointment at a junior college in Oklahoma. The next year he taught in Nebraska; the year after it was Colorado—time spent hoping that temporary appointments would become permanent.

But at the end of each academic year all he got was a warm handshake and a goodbye.

"We've had good reports on your teaching," one department chairman told him on his last day.

"Then let me stay and teach."

The department chairman would not look directly at him. "What we're really looking for is someone who can conduct a research program."

"I can do that if I don't have so many classes to teach."

The chairman looked at his watch. It was almost time for lunch. "It's not just doing research. We need someone who can bring in research money."

"Give me a chance."

"We can't. The man you replaced has tenure and he's coming back from his sabbatical in July. We don't have room for you. But I'll be happy to write a nice letter of reference."

One day he realized he was thirty-three years old with two children and a wife who had done nothing but pack and unpack since their marriage.

The bubble had burst. It was time to grow up.

The nation didn't need him after all.

They moved to South Dakota, where Janice's brother Ted, who was still in the Air Force, offered to make Eric a partner in running an Orange Julius franchise in a new shopping mall. The plan was that after Ted was passed over for major, he would get out of the service and work full-time with Eric.

The Air Force, characteristically uncooperative, promoted Ted to major three months later. He was transferred to New York, leaving Eric with the business. He had been there ever since.

The phone interrupted his thinking.

"Is this Lawn Doctor?" a lady asked. "I wish you were here to see the dandelions in my yard."

"When did you sign up with us?"

"Four days ago. You said you'd be by to spray."

"The wind's slowed me down. I can't spray when it's windy."

"It's not windy now," she said icily.

"No, it's not. I have some other appointments. How about first thing next week?"

"By then the dandelions will have taken over the whole yard."

"If you mow the lawn, it won't be so noticeable. I'll be out Monday or Tuesday. And our work is guaranteed, so don't worry."

"All right," she said.

While thumbing through the high school annual, he found a photograph of Ann and him on the night of the junior-senior prom.

Ann was the first girl he ever dated—the one who waved him off on his mission. The one who later sent him a Dear John letter.

He hadn't heard much about her except that she was married and living in Ranger. Maybe she'll be at the reunion, he thought. I just hope her husband isn't rich or famous.

He closed the pages of the annual and started on his list of call-backs.

The first was President Baxter, the stake president, a highly successful lawyer who had from the beginning made Eric feel like an unprepared defense witness.

Sometimes Eric wondered what the second priority of a bishop was. Every topic his leaders stressed—from welfare projects to youth to activation to missionary work to teacher development to building maintenance—they were all listed as a bishop's responsibility. "The success of this program rests with the bishop" had by now become a familiar phrase.

"Bishop," President Baxter said after a few seconds of idle conversation, "we'd like to take Brother Williamson as a member of the stake high council."

Inwardly Eric moaned.

"I'm very reluctant to see that happen, president."

"Why?"

"He's our scoutmaster. He's been there for only a year, and we're just starting to get some advancement in rank from our boys." He paused, debating whether or not to use the ploy. Why not? "I'm sure you realize that the Aaronic Priesthood is the first responsibility of a bishop."

There was a long pause. "Bishop, how can the stake assist the wards if you won't allow us to staff our organization?"

"What about Second Ward?" he asked. "They never seem to have anyone called to a stake position."

"No, he has to come from your ward this time."

"Anyone but our scoutmaster."

"Do you have any recommendations?" President Baxter asked.

Eric cringed. It was like asking which arm he wanted cut off. Don't take my elders quorum president or my counselors, he thought.

"Not right off, president. I'd have to discuss it with my counselors."

"All right. You'll be at church on Sunday?"

"No—Janice and I are going to a high school reunion."

"Good idea. You've looked tired lately. Oh, one other thing—your bee project. The wards should have applied some Terramycin to the hives by now. Do you know if your ward has done that?"

"Let me check on it, president, and I'll get back to you."

Three more phone calls for Lawn Doctor, one more to arrange working schedules for Orange Julius, a call-back to one of his tall, lanky ward members who couldn't understand why youth weren't allowed to play basketball when the women were doing their aerobic exercises.

Then the phone rang for him.

"We're just passing through town, and we looked in the yellow pages under churches, and doggone if we didn't find you listed there. We need food—hamburger meat, buns, chips, mustard, pickles, and eggs. It's for me and my friend Bunny. My name's Ace."

"Are you members of the Church?"

"No, but I have relatives who are."

"What church do you belong to?"

"Just a minute," he said, then yelled, "Hey Bunny, he wants to know what church we belong to. What'll I tell him?"

A muffled answer from Bunny to Ace.

"We think all churches are good," Ace said into the phone.

"Well, what church do you go to?"

"Hey, now he wants to know what church we go to."

Pause.

Ace named a church.

"I suggest you contact them," Eric said. "They'll probably help you out. Don't you have any food at all?"

"Beans—that's all. You ever tried to live on beans for a month?"

"I lived on beans for four years," Eric said, remembering graduate school.

Ace made a crude comment about beans.

Eric gave him the phone number of the other church.

"You're actually going to turn us away? You're going to refuse to help us?"

"That's right," Eric said.

Long pause while Ace conferred with Bunny.

"Wait a minute. I didn't want to tell you this, but Bunny's developed an allergy to beans. The doctor says she'll die if she eats any more. It's pretty serious."

"Tell the pastor that. I'm sure he'll help out—especially for something so serious as that."

"Don't hang up! I just noticed your last name is Turner. Are you any relation to Bill Newby from Greybull, Wyoming?"

Eric paused. Bill Newby was his dad's cousin. Eric as a young boy on a vacation vaguely remembered visiting the Newby ranch.

"Maybe I am. Why?"

"Well, Bill Newby is my dad."

Eric paused. It might be true. He could remember some kids he had played with while he was there for the day or two they stayed with the Newbys.

"Hey, small world, hey? Now can we get the food, cousin?"

"I can't give it to you from church funds."

"That's all right. We don't care where it comes from.

Give it to us from your own money. We'll be right over."

Ace hung up.

Eric went upstairs. Janice was in their room packing. He packed his things too.

He noticed two cartons on the bed. "What's that?"

She cleared her throat. "That? Oh, it's just something I thought we would take on our trip."

"But what is it?"

"Girl Scout mints in this box and Girl Scout cookies in the other one."

"You're kidding."

"You always say how much you like 'em."

He read the printing on each box. There were twelve packages in each box.

"Why do we need twelve boxes of Girl Scout cookies and mints?"

"I knew you wouldn't understand."

"I'll try. Why did you buy twelve boxes of Girl Scout cookies and twelve boxes of mints?"

She smiled sheepishly. "A few months ago, there was this sweet girl who came to the door. She was selling Girl Scout cookies. Eric, she was so shy. She didn't even look up at me. And by then the neighborhood already had three or four girls come by, so I knew nobody had bought anything from her. She said, 'You don't want to buy any Girl Scout cookies, do you?'

"Well, I thought back to the times we lived in apartments while you were in school and how I never had any money for anything extra—and all the boys and girls I had turned down with their raffles and pancake suppers and Boy Scout expeditions. I looked at that little girl, and before I could think, I told her I'd take all she had. Eric, she looked up at me and I'll never forget what she said."

"What did she say?"

"She said, 'Really?' And I said yes. She ran yelling to her mom and together they brought the two cases to the door."

"How much was it?" he asked.

She smiled weakly. "If you think of it in terms of a year's supply, I think it'll rest easier with you."

"A year's supply of Girl Scout cookies?" he asked.

"And mints too."

The phone rang.

Eric answered. It was Dale Warren, a freshman at the local college.

"I'm going to Texas!"

"You got your mission call?"

"I got it today. I report to the Missionary Training Center in a month for language training."

Eric paused. "You have to have language training for a mission in Texas?"

"I'll be working with the Spanish-speaking people there. I'm going over to tell Noelle now. She'll be so excited. Can we come over tonight and show you the letter and talk to you?"

"Well, not tonight, Dale. My wife and I are going to a high school reunion in Montana."

"Where at?"

"Well, it's at a ski lodge about fifty miles from Ranger."

"You mean Frosty Hollow?"

"Yes."

"I know where that is. I've skied there before. It's not very far."

"It's pretty far, Dale. Besides I can talk to you and Noelle on Monday when we get back."

A minute later he hung up the phone. From nowhere his fourteen-year-old daughter rushed over to save the phone from the awful fate of being unused.

"Hi, Kim," he said.

"Hi, Dad," she replied, dialing her number.

"How are things?"

"Fine."

She finished dialing.

"Let's have a nice talk like this again sometime," he said.

The line was busy. Kim disgustedly hung up. The phone rang. She answered it eagerly, but it was for her father. It was his Relief Society president with problems to talk about.

Janice started carrying things to the car.

"I'm sorry," he whispered after one of her trips.

"It's all right. I knew it'd be this way."

The phone conversation continued. "Bishop, do you realize you budgeted us only fifteen dollars for our luncheon next week? How do I feed forty women on fifteen dollars?"

He heard voices on the front steps. Janice was saying, "He's on the phone now, but if you'd like to come in and wait . . ."

The screen door opened and two gorillas walked in the house.

One of them had no shirt on and was wearing a faded, greasy denim vest, exposing a massive hairy chest and large silver chain hanging from his neck. He had a long, snarly, reddish beard. He wore grease-stained jeans and boots.

The second one had a black leather jacket partially open, with no shirt underneath, and a leather cap. His chest was covered with tattoos, and he had a knife tucked into one of his boots.

Then two girls came in. They looked identical, with T-shirts and jeans and long wind-tossed hair and a diffuse far-away expression.

"I'm Eric's second cousin," the one with the neck-chain said. "My name's Ace. And this is Bunny. And these are some friends we met on the road. We call him Bones and her Starlight."

"How nice," Janice said pleasantly. "Would you like some Girl Scout cookies and some lemonade?"

"Sister Goodwin," Eric said, "I'm hanging up now."

"No, please! Just let me ask one more question. It'll only take a minute."

Janice sent Brent to the car for a package of cookies

while she went to the kitchen. A minute later she came out with a tray for their guests. Four glasses were full, with a pitcher for seconds. Bones didn't understand the arrangement—he grabbed the pitcher and drank from it. They chug-a-lugged the lemonade, then attacked the cookies.

"It's certainly been a warm day, hasn't it?" Janice said.

Bones let fly a barrage of swear words. In essence his reply was that, yes indeed, it had been warm.

"Would you care for some more lemonade?" Janice asked.

"What we really want is a little hamburger, buns, chips, a package of lunch meat, and some eggs."

"And a shower," Bunny said.

Eric was still on the phone. "Sister Goodwin, please. I've got to hang up. My home's been invaded by a motorcycle gang. I'll call you back later."

Eric hung up and hurried to the living room.

Ace was sitting in Eric's chair watching TV.

"Hi, cousin," Ace grinned.

Bones pulled out a switchblade and started digging the grease from his fingernails.

Janice came into the living room with a sack full of food.

"I'm afraid the hamburger is still frozen. Oh, I threw in a loaf of banana nut bread for you and your wives."

"Wives!" Ace laughed. Bunny laughed. Bones laughed. Starlight laughed.

Eric did not laugh. He felt intimidated.

At the same time he wondered where Janice had been hiding the banana nut bread.

He marched into the kitchen, grabbed the frozen carp, came back, and plopped it into their bag. "Here's something a little extra for you," he said.

"What about a shower?" Bunny asked.

"I'm afraid we can't help you out on that," Janice said. "You see, we're going away for the weekend. In fact, we were just leaving when you came."

"Where you going?" Bones asked.

"Frosty Hollow Ski Lodge."

"I've been there," Bunny said.

"Oh yeah, what for?" Ace asked.

"Skiing."

"Makes sense," Bones said, tipping the pitcher up for a drink and dumping ice cubes all over the floor. "So you'll be gone all weekend, huh?"

"I'm afraid so," Janice said.

Eric cringed. "Janice, may I please have a word with you in the kitchen?"

They went to the kitchen and shut the door.

"Janice, what are you doing? Why don't you just ask them to steal everything from us while we're gone?"

"He's your cousin, isn't he?"

"Maybe he is, but we don't have to invite him to rob us while we're gone, do we? Now let's just get 'em out of here so we can be on our way. We'll miss the registration and family social if we don't leave now."

They returned to the living room. Ace was reading a *Time* magazine. Bones was lying on the couch, his boots dirtying the armrest. Starlight was eating a box of Girl Scout mints and scratching herself.

"Where's the other girl?" Eric asked.

"Taking a shower."

"In my house?" Eric roared.

"Hey—not so loud," Ace complained. "I can't hear the news."

Eric and Janice went to the bathroom door. They could hear the shower running. "Janice, get her out of the shower."

"How, dear?"

The door was locked. They could hear her singing a song with unique lyrics.

Brent came in from the car. "Dad, when are we leaving?"

"As soon as we get the woman out of our shower," Eric muttered. "Get away, son—don't listen to her sing."

"You won't forget to find someone to take care of my gerbil, will you?"

"Don't worry about the gerbil," Janice reassured him.

There was nothing to do but wait. Eric stormed to his office and sat glumly at his desk.

The phone rang.

"Bishop, what's your favorite color?" a ward member asked.

"I don't have a favorite color," he mumbled.

"Oh, come now, you must have a favorite color. Everyone has a favorite color."

He looked at the Lawn Doctor sign and said, "Green."

He heard the shower stop.

"Any particular reason for the question?" Eric asked.

"No, no—just wondering. 'Bye."

The next call was from a member of the stake high council. "Bishop, I've been asked to work with your ward to encourage members to have gardens this year. You know, one of your most important responsibilities as a bishop is to teach your ward members to have gardens and store food."

"Brother Bentley, it's the middle of June. Isn't it a little late to encourage people to have gardens?"

"I've been out of town a lot lately. I'd like you to phone every family in your ward and get me a list by Tuesday of how many have gardens, approximately how many square feet are planted, what the expected production of corn, radishes, lettuce, tomatoes, and so on will be this year, as well as the breakdown on the average cost of fertilizer, equipment, and seeds."

"You want that by Tuesday?"

"I should think you'd want to do it, bishop. The success of your ward's efforts to store food rests with you."

"Brother Bentley, I don't see how I can possibly get all that information by Tuesday."

Brother Bentley was not happy. "What are you going to do when the stores are all out of food, and your ward members come to you, begging for a morsel of food? What are you going to do then?"

Eric thought a minute, then answered. "I'll give them pickled beets."

He went upstairs. Ace and Bones were outside giving motorcycle rides to the kids in the neighborhood.

Doug and Cathy had stayed in the car and eaten mints. They were both a chocolate mess.

Bunny came into the living room wearing a pair of Janice's tan slacks. Starlight was now wearing a white blouse over her T-shirt.

"That's such terrific body lotion," Bunny said. "Are you sure it's all right if I take it with me?"

"Of course. Look, I know how dry your skin must get riding across the country on a motorcycle."

"You folks are really nice," Bunny said.

"I didn't want a shower," Starlight said. "It attracts mosquitoes if you're too clean."

They all walked outside.

"What about my gerbil?" Brent asked.

"Later, Brent," Eric said.

Bunny got on the back of Ace's chopper. Starlight climbed behind Bones on his Harley-Davidson.

"Now you come back and see us when you're in the area again," Janice called out brightly.

"You can count on it," Ace replied.

They rode off into the late afternoon sun.

Ten minutes later, Eric and Janice closed up the house and were on their way. Just before pulling into the driveway of the Roberts' home where their children were to stay, Doug let out a string of swear words.

Janice gasped.

Eric slammed on the brakes.

"Don't let me ever hear you say that again, young man!"

"Uncle Ace says that," his seven-year-old said.

"He's not our uncle!"

"What about my gerbil?" Brent asked.

"Later, Brent!"

Sister Roberts, smiling warmly, started across the lawn toward them.

Eric turned around to face Doug. "Now listen to me. You must never say those words again. Especially not this weekend—and especially not to Sister Roberts. Do you understand me?"

Sister Roberts leaned down to say hello.

"Okay, Daddy," Doug agreed.

Finally they were free.

A few miles from home, just outside the stake boundaries, Eric stopped and ordered some food at a drive-in. While they waited for their order, he removed the car seat that for the past fifteen years had kept them separated in the car. Then he gave Janice a nicely wrapped gift.

"To our weekend," he said.

"Oh, Eric, how sweet."

He scowled. "Don't say sweet—it reminds me of beehives."

She opened the package. It was a lacy pink nightgown.

"Janice, I love you."

"It's lovely. After I've had the baby, I'll wear it."

"How about tonight?"

"I'm so big now. Can it wait till I feel more glamorous?"

"Please."

She smiled. "We'll see."

They ate and started out again.

"Eric," she said, "why are we going to this reunion of yours?"

"I don't know—just to renew some friendships, I guess."

"That's all?"

"Sure, why?"

"Will Ann be there?" she asked softly.

CHAPTER TWO

1959

Ann stomped into her room, slammed the door, angrily removed her blue dress, threw it on the floor, and glared at the other dresses in the closet. The last words of her father still rang in her ears—"Young lady, you are *not* wearing that dress on a date! Now go find something a little more modest or you're not going at all—and that's final!"

She found a flowered print and put it on. It made her look like a little girl, and she hated it.

She stared with disgust at her hair. It looked as if she'd been in an explosion in a hair spray factory.

The doorbell rang. She quickly zipped the dress and hurried to the bathroom for one last try with her hair.

Shaking the spray can, she sprayed it on thick.

"What do you do?" she heard her father quiz Eric in the living room.

"Do? I go to school."

"Yes, but what are you going to do?"

"Tonight?" Eric asked, sounding threatened.

"No—in your life. What are you going to do in your life?"

"Work, I guess."

"Work where, though?" her father shot back.

"I don't know."

"You should find out. At your age I knew what I was going to do. If you don't decide now, when will you?"

"I'll decide tonight," Eric quickly promised.

"Take your time," her father warned. "Don't rush into anything."

"I won't decide tonight. I'll take my time."

"But soon."

"Tomorrow."

Ann brushed her hair faster and faster, hoping to make it to the living room before her father ruined her entire life.

"You'll think this is dumb probably," Eric said, "but sometimes I think I'd like to be a sculptor."

"No, no—that's not what you want to do," her father said. "You'll never earn a decent living doing that. Look, if you want a little advice, have you ever thought about the methane produced from animal waste?"

Ann gasped. The lipstick jumped the track along her lip contour.

"What?" Eric asked.

"The gases from sewage. I think it's a gold mine that's being overlooked, don't you?"

"I guess so."

Now her hair felt like steel wool because of too much hair spray.

"Another thing," her father continued. "We've got to stop the Russians from controlling space. They have a head start on us with Sputnik, but we're going to beat 'em because we're smarter. We've got you young people with good minds for science and math. That's what makes America great—and don't you ever forget it."

The brush was stuck in her hair. She yanked on it, and the pain in her scalp made her eyes water. Suddenly the brush broke free, and her hand struck the mirror.

She looked at herself in the mirror. A long heap of hair stuck straight up from her head. She tried to mat it down as best as she could, but it kept bouncing up.

She sucked on her knuckle where her hand had hit the mirror, patted her head, and wiped away the tears so they wouldn't wreck her eye makeup.

Her mother moved slowly along the hall to the bathroom, using her walker to support the arthritis-ravaged joints. She painfully got to the bathroom, looked in, and told Ann she looked just fine.

A minute later Ann blew her nose and walked into the living room.

As quickly as they could, with her father still lecturing on sewage treatment, Eric and Ann fled the house.

He drove his older brother's car. He turned on the radio. It played for a minute, then stopped.

When it quits, his brother had told him before the date, just tap it once or twice. At the next stoplight, Eric tapped the radio with his fist. Nothing happened. He casually put his foot against the dashboard and kicked it lightly. Nothing happened. *That's no way to treat a radio,* Ann thought.

The next time they stopped, he put both feet against it and kicked as hard as he could, smashing out the glass and breaking off both plastic knobs.

I must remember not to get him mad at me, she thought.

They drove in silence until Eric, with almost superhuman effort, tried to start a conversation.

"You know," he chuckled, "my ten-year-old brother is really a chess nut."

Ann stared straight ahead and tried to figure out his meaning. *His brother is a chestnut?*

"Oh really," she said pleasantly.

She realized she was nervously patting her hair unicorn down, and that he was looking at her strangely.

"Do you play chess?" he asked.

"No."

Another eternity of silence.

Her head itched. She wondered if it was true what they said in the magazines about dandruff—that if she scratched, he'd be disgusted and take her home.

They had planned on a movie, but when they rounded the corner, they realized the theater had changed movies, and the new movie was one they should not see.

They drove around town looking for another movie, but he didn't like any of the others.

"What would you like to do?" he finally asked.

"I don't know—whatever you think."

"Really, if there's anything you'd like to do, just say the word."

Silence.

"Do you have much interest in steam locomotives?" he finally asked.

Why me? she thought.

"I guess I've never really thought about it before," she said.

"I know where one is. I think you'd really enjoy seeing it."

An hour for a bath, she thought, *two hours on my dumb hair—for this?*

"There's nothing quite like a steam locomotive. Ever since I was a kid . . . "

He's still a kid, she thought.

" . . . when I had an electric train, I've been interested in steam locomotives."

She smiled brightly as if she cared.

"My dad started me right on H-O gauge. You see, the thing in model railroading is to make everything as realistic as possible. We even painted grass on the plywood. And we made a papier-mache tunnel for the train to go through."

I wonder how much time my social studies homework will take, she thought.

"And I carved a tiny mountain goat out of wood for the top of the tunnel."

He's as boring as cold mush, she thought.

"Isn't that interesting?" she said cheerily.

"I was only in the fourth grade at the time, but many people have complimented me on my mountain goat. I even carved little horns for its head."

She reached up to check her hair. It had sprung out again.

"In Scouts, I even got a merit badge for wood carving. Someday I might be a famous sculptor and do a full-scale mountain goat. Wouldn't that be something?"

She deliberately reached up with both hands and began wildly scratching her head.

Look at me! she thought. *I have dandruff! I'm in a room ten minutes and it looks like a snowstorm. Look at me scratch. Doesn't that disgust you? Please be disgusted and take me home.*

"One year for Christmas, I even carved a horse for my father."

She slumped in her seat. "Oh," she muttered.

"I bet a lot of sculptors started off with just something small, but they kept practicing. Or maybe I'll go into science. I'm good in math. Maybe I could help us put a man on the moon and help our country beat the Russians."

They pulled in front of the sugar beet factory. A small steam locomotive pulled several freight cars.

"Well, what do you think?" he said proudly.

Big deal, she thought—*a choo-choo train.*

"Really," she said brightly.

"You know, the history of steam locomotives is really the history of America."

Silence.

"I don't know if you've ever thought about it like that before."

Like what? she thought. *An hour for a bath, two hours on my ratty hair . . .*

Eric gave up and just watched the locomotive.

The train engineer saw them, waved, got down, and walked over to them.

"She's a beaut, right?" he said to Eric.

"Yeah! I love to watch her puff clouds of steam and belch in the night."

Why a she? Ann thought. *I know plenty of guys who belch in the night.*

"I have a subscription to *Model Railroading,*" Eric announced proudly.

"No kidding? C'mon, I'll give you both a ride."

No way, she thought.

"Wow!" Eric said.

The three of them climbed into the locomotive cab. It was hot and covered with soot and grease.

An hour for a bath, she thought, *two hours on my dumb hair, an hour to argue with my parents about the blue dress . . .*

"I can't believe we're actually here, can you?" Eric asked.

"No, I can't," she answered, thinking how ugly it all was and that she should stand in the middle to avoid getting her dress dirty.

"Now to get us going, just move this lever forward a little. Care to try it?"

Eric threw the handle and the train jerked forward, throwing Ann against the back partition. To keep from falling, she grabbed a post and hung on.

"Not quite that much," the engineer said to Eric. They paid no attention to her.

I'm not going to look at my dress now, she thought. *I'm just going to worry about staying alive.*

"How old is she?" Eric asked.

"She was built in '38."

My mother will say, "You should have told him you're not allowed to ride in coal cars with that dress."

"It pulled a commuter train in Chicago till it went on the auction block. That's when we got it."

My father will say, What did you do to encourage him to take you to the train?

"I have to blow the whistle at the next crossing," the engineer said. "Want to do it?"

"Do I?" Eric said. He turned for the first time to see Ann hanging to the post.

He paused to look at her. "Ann, I don't think you should hang onto that. You might get dirty."

He tried to pull her away, but she grabbed tighter.

The engineer yelled, "Somebody better blow the whistle now!"

"Ann, if you let go, I'll let you blow the whistle—but first you have to let go."

Ann shook her head.

"Okay then, I'll blow the whistle."

He blew the whistle.

Eric was ecstatic. "Just think—I'm on a locomotive that pulled trains in Chicago!"

Chicago? Ann thought. *We're going to Chicago? I'll get back in two weeks, covered with soot—my parents will ask where I've been. I'll tell 'em I went to Chicago on a sugar beet train, and they'll say that I should have phoned if I knew I was going to be late. I'll tell 'em there wasn't a phone and they'll say that isn't any excuse—if I really cared about them waiting up for two weeks, I could've found a phone . . . Or we'll crash and burn, especially with Eric driving. If I die, I hope they bury me in the blue dress . . . People will come and see me in the coffin and say, "I don't think it's that immodest."*

They reached their destination, a huge pile of sugar beets. "It'll take 'em a while to load up again. If you can't wait, you can walk back along the tracks."

"We'll stay," Eric said quickly.

"I have to go," Ann said.

"It's only eight o'clock."

"My parents have a rule about riding freight trains after eight o'clock," she lied.

"You actually want to leave now?"

"Yes, I do."

He sulked as they walked back.

What will I say, she thought, *when they ask me how my first date went? I could say it was a sweet date and not mention the sugar beets. I could say it was the kind of date where you hear loud whistles. I could say it was a very moving experience . . .*

She felt a large drop of rain—and then another. Suddenly it was raining very hard.

"Run for it!" he shouted, pulling at her arm.

"I can't go very fast in these shoes."

"Then take 'em off and run barefoot!"

He took one last look, then abandoned her.

Reluctantly she took off her shoes and ran after him.

This is a date? she thought. *I waited sixteen years for this?*

Half a block from the car, she stumbled on a cross tie and drove a sliver into her foot.

"Ow!" she cried out.

"Now what's wrong?" He turned disgustedly to look at her.

"I've got a sliver in my foot!"

"Limp on one foot then," he said, leaving her to make it to the car as best she could.

I hate you, she thought, limping toward the car.

She finally opened the car door and stepped in. Instinctively she felt her hair. At least the unicorn was gone.

"Let me look at your foot," he said.

"No, it's all right."

"Just let me look at it."

He crouched on the floorboard, turned on the dome light, and examined her foot. Without warning he took a pocketknife and cut away the bottom of her nylon stocking.

He's crazy, she thought. *Look at him with that knife. But I mustn't get him mad at me. Just keep calm and keep repeating to myself . . . remember the radio, remember the radio, remember the radio . . .*

He made an incision, folded back the skin, and pulled out the splinter.

"I did it! Look at that, would you?" He waved the splinter in front of her. "That was in your foot!"

She ran her fingers through her wet hair.

In a minute he started the engine and tried to pull out, but they were stuck in the mud.

"Stuck," he said after several attempts.

"Oh," she said politely.

"One of us should get out and push."

She looked at him in shock. "One of us?"

"Yes, one of us should push, and the other—the one who knows how to shift gears—should drive."

She stared at the rain and wished with all her heart that dandruff was contagious.

"I don't think I want to push," she said politely.

There was a long pause.

"Well," he said, "if you don't push, then I'll have to walk through the rain to a telephone and call my dad to pick us up."

"Oh," she said.

They each tried to wait the other out. Finally he gave up and went to call his dad.

When his father arrived, they decided to leave the car until morning. They left in the family car.

"Well, how was your date?" his father asked.

Ann stared straight ahead and clamped her teeth together.

"It was okay," Eric said, "until we had to leave the locomotive."

"You know," his father said, "I envy you kids your youth. To be young and not tied down with responsibilities. I just hope you cherish these golden experiences."

Her mouth dropped open.

Golden experiences? These are golden experiences?

* * * * *

Beginning in their junior year, Eric and Ann went steady. Their time alone was more like two travelers huddling together to escape the ravages of a mountain storm.

Ann's storm swirled around her mother's arthritis, which had gradually sucked away all useful functions of her limbs. Ann, being the only child at home, was called upon to perform most of the household chores as well as some practical nursing.

Their relationship began the spring of their junior

year during a Sunday School class picnic that involved a hike to a waterfall deep in the forest fifty miles from home. Eric was asked to carry a watermelon, and so he was traveling slower than the others in the class. He ended up walking with Ann.

He had been mumbling to her about Einstein's theory of relativity. It was something he often inflicted on others who'd listen. " . . . and in the rocket ship, time actually slows down. And maybe if the rocket ship went at the speed of light, time would stop."

"I know how time can slow down," she said.

"You do?"

"During the summer I have to take care of my mother. All we do is watch TV and wait for the time for another pain pill. Time really slows down in the summer."

They stopped to rest.

"She's never going to get any better," Ann said. "All the pills do is stop the pain and give her an ulcer. But my dad keeps on day after day, doing the chores I can't get done. He never complains. And my mom, she's just withering away. Her fingers are all twisted and bent. And nobody can stop it. It just keeps at her all the time."

"I'm sorry."

"Me too—sorry for her, sorry for my dad, sorry for me."

They walked in silence for a while.

"I've never told this to anyone," she said, "but sometimes I hate her for being sick. She's ruining my life. I can't be in the pep club because I have to go home after school and watch her until Daddy gets home. I guess you don't think very much of me for saying that, do you."

"I can see how you'd feel that way, Ann."

"Sometimes more than anything I'd like to wear a pep club sweater on Fridays like the really popular girls do. And have boys call me up on the telephone."

"I guess everyone'd like to be popular."

"Do you think a guy would ever be interested in me?"

"Sure, why not?"

"I want boys to like me. But how will they even know I exist if I spend my whole life cooped up in our house with my mother?"

"I like you, sort of," he said. "If you want, sometime I could go to your house and we could talk or something."

"Would you want to do that?"

"Why not? I don't have anything else to do most of the time."

She reached over and touched his arm lightly. "Maybe we could be friends and help each other."

Eric began visiting her. They became good friends that summer.

"I like to kiss you," she whispered in his ear one evening in September in a car parked outside her home.

"Me too," he said dreamily.

"But maybe it's for the wrong reason," she added. "When we kiss, I forget about my mom. And when I'm home taking care of her, all I do is look forward to when you'll be there with me. Sometimes I think about us leaving and never coming back. Just driving forever. Do you ever think about that?"

"No—but I do like to kiss you."

"Would you say you need me or love me?"

He pulled away from her. "Huh?"

"I read about it in a magazine. Some couples get together because they need each other, and that's not good. We're not supposed to need each other—but I need you. If you didn't come by after school, I don't know what I'd do."

"I think I love you."

"You're not sure?"

"You're the first girl I've ever dated, so I don't have anyone else to compare you with, but I'm pretty sure though. Yes, I do, Ann. I love you."

"Would you say you love me more than need me or need me more than love me?"

"I don't know. Maybe I need you too."

"Why do you need me?"

"Because you like me, and most people in school don't."

"Why don't they like you?"

"I don't know—maybe because I don't like them."

"Oh," she said quietly.

"Ann, what's it like in a girls' locker room?"

"How do you mean?"

"Today after gym class, everyone was standing around getting dressed, and four guys started a towel fight, and they ran around yelling and banging on the lockers and flicking towels at each other. One guy knocked over a whole row of lockers. You can't believe the noise. And I'm trying to get my socks right side out before I put 'em on. They tell dirty jokes and talk about the girls they date, and they brag about how much beer they can drink."

"It's not like that in the girls' locker room," she said.

"They make it sound like to be a man, you have to do those things."

"I don't think swearing and telling dirty jokes and destroying property is masculine."

"But what is?"

"The way you make me feel safe and protected when we go out, the way you hold me, the way you have so much hair on your arms, and the muscles in your arms. And even the way you bless the sacrament every Sunday. I think gentleness can be masculine."

"Why don't people like me?" he asked.

"Eric, I know you mean well, but every time anybody gets near you, you talk over their heads. People don't like knowing how stupid they are, and just because it's exciting to you, it isn't to others. I think you should talk about what they're interested in. Maybe later you can tell them about science, but maybe you'd learn something if you'd let them talk about what they're interested in."

He thought about it and then said, "But what if all they're interested in is dirty jokes?"

"Nobody's interested in just that."

"I can tell you've never heard 'em talk in the locker room."

"Maybe you should learn to talk about sports."

"Sports? Why?"

"To make friends. You could get a subscription to *Sports Illustrated* and talk about what you read each week. You don't even have to know how to play. I read all the time at home. For instance, do you know how to get gum out of clothes? All you do is put it in the freezer and wait. Then you just scrape off the frozen gum. I read that in *Better Homes and Gardens* yesterday while I was taking care of my mother. I read things like that and collect them in a scrapbook. You never know when they'll come in handy. That's the value of reading. You can read about sports and then you'll have something to talk about—even to guys in gym class."

"Okay, I'll try it. Thanks. You're the only person I can talk to about things like this."

"Eric, maybe also you should get involved in student government. Why don't you try for president of science club? Then you'd be on student council too."

"Why?"

"That way people'd get to know you better and you could be more friendly."

"Nobody'd ever vote for me."

"Now see, that's negative thinking, and we have to help each other get rid of negative thinking. I have a book I'll loan you. I just know you can do it."

With her coaching, he won the election.

Ann helped him with trying to be more friendly. He forced himself to start talking to kids in school. He acquired two subscriptions that got him through—*Sports Illustrated* and *Modern Cycle*.

He found he couldn't get along without Ann.

"I love you, Ann—more than I need you." This was said in a car parked on a hill overlooking their town.

"And I love you, Eric."

"I've never been in love before. It's very nice."

He kissed her again. And again. And again.

"I think we'd better go home now," she said.

"Already? Just a few minutes more."

"No, I don't think so, Eric. I think it would be best if you took me home now."

"What for?"

"Because you might lose control of youself. Guys can't control themselves very well. I read about it yesterday."

"You read too much," he said, nibbling her ear. "Besides, I wasn't losing control. It was just kissing."

"No use taking chances, is there? What if something went wrong and you didn't get to go on your mission?"

"I'm not sure I even want to go on a mission."

"Oh, sure, you've got to go. You're supposed to go."

"But I love you. I want to marry you someday. And if I went on a mission, you might marry somebody else."

"I won't. I'll wait. No matter what happens, I'll always love you—because you're helping me through a difficult time in my life. Promise me you'll go on a mission. I could never marry someone who hadn't served a mission."

"I'll think about it."

He drove her home. They went inside and popped popcorn, then went into the living room and ate and watched TV with her parents. Her mother was in her usual position, sitting propped up in an easy chair, the wheelchair not far away, a TV tray of pills and water glasses, and dishes of applesauce used with the pills. Her fingers curled inward into an unmanageable shape. Her father was working on still another version of a bicycle that could be used for therapy for his wife. Over the past year, he had designed several exercise devices for her. They would have worked well, except the arthritis couldn't be stopped. The apparatus would end up being used once, causing more pain, then politely discarded until the next attempt.

Her mother started to cough. She sounded terrible.

"I need another pill," she said.

Ann started to get up, but her father stopped her. "No, you've got Eric here. I can get it."

For some reason, as if a photo had been made on his brain, the image that night had burned into Eric's mind, and he never forgot it. Ann's mother touching those deformed fingers, as though by some magic of touch they might come to life again; the tray of pills; the black-and-white TV showing Sergeant Bilko and his manic humor; the room holding a never-used exercise bike and a homemade wheelchair because the kind you rent was too wide for the narrow halls of their house; Ann's mother rocking back and forth, staring at the TV screen; the canned laughter from some long-dead studio audience; Ann putting another handful of popcorn in her mouth as if nothing was wrong, as if every American family had this to cope with.

Suddenly Eric wanted to rescue Ann from her prison, to drive away as she said, to get married and live on the beaches of California and go swimming every day and never come back to this home.

He reached over and took her hand and squeezed it tightly.

Her mother started coughing again.

"We'd better ask the doctor about that cough tomorrow when we see him," Ann's father said, as he gave her the pill and helped her drink the water.

The next day Ann's mother was admitted to the hospital with pneumonia, and a week later she died. It seemed a cruel irony for her to die of pneumonia when for so many years arthritis had been the enemy.

Eric stood with Ann and her father as they viewed the body a few hours before the funeral, and they all hugged each other and cried until there were no more tears. They got through the funeral because of numbness, because nature is kind enough to shelter us with shock when some things cannot be assimilated all at once.

She was buried during a snowstorm, but there were many flowers at the graveside, and Ann's father said that was good because she always liked flowers. That night Ann and Eric went back to the grave. The flowers were frozen and covered with snow.

The next August when he turned nineteen, Eric went on his mission. He left Ann with an engagement ring.

One of her letters came in February. She was a freshman at BYU. The letter read: "My dad wrote and says he's getting along okay. He's started to see another woman. They knew each other in high school, and he says he likes her very much. He might even ask her to marry him. If he does, I'll never be able to go home again. It just wouldn't ever be the same."

He never forgot that letter.

There was one more letter from her that he never forgot.

CHAPTER THREE

Eric and Janice arrived at Frosty Hollow Lodge at ten o'clock that night. The lobby contained a large poster welcoming the class of '61, as well as a registration table. Behind the table sat a slim blonde with a lowcut dress. When she saw Eric, she stood up and kissed him on the cheek. "Eric! You look terrific! I'm so glad to see you."

"Hi there," he said, unable to remember anyone in his class who looked the way she did.

"Is this your wife?" the woman asked.

"Oh, yes, this is my wife."

"I'm so glad to meet you. Eric and I had so much fun together in high school. You be sure and have him tell you about it."

"I certainly will," Janice promised.

"You're looking good, Eric," she said. "What a tan—I'd say you either golf or play tennis."

"Is your husband here?" Eric asked, trying desperately to come up with some connection to remind him who she was.

"No—I'm not married now. My divorce came through last month."

"Oh, I see."

"Oh, Eric, it's so good to see you. All that time we spent together in our senior year—it was a good time, wasn't it?"

Eric could feel Janice's glare melting his shirt.

"Oh, sure, I guess so. In a wholesome way, of course, it was a fun time."

She laughed. "Oh, Eric, you're still a kidder."

"I am?"

She handed him a schedule for the reunion as well as a brief biography of most of the reunion participants. "Now be sure and save some time so we can get together and talk about old times, won't you."

They walked away from the table.

"Who's she?" Janice asked.

"I don't know."

" 'All that time we spent together in our senior year,' " she mimicked.

"I'm telling you the truth. There was nobody in our class who looked like that. And I'm sure I never dated her. I would've remembered."

"Unless you're trying to forget," she said quietly.

The lodge had been built in the thirties, but things had gone steadily downhill until the early sixties, when a New Jersey corporation had built a large ski area just a mile away. With that, business picked up. A modern hotel complex had recently been added just across from the old lodge.

The lodge had a large lounge area with rock fireplace and hand-hewn furniture. Eric had been assigned one of the rooms above the lobby in the old hotel. It was a simple room, built before plastic, with a large throw rug on the oak floor and a double bed that creaked.

There was no TV in the room.

The handle of the ancient toilet required jiggling after each use to stop the water from continually running into the bowl. The bath was large and old and yellowing with age. The bathroom mirror had a crack running diagonally across it.

But the room did have a view of a large snow-capped mountain peak that was awesome in its sterile white beauty.

They unpacked silently. One overhead light made

the room seem like a prison cell, but the reading lamp next to the bed helped soften the lighting.

Janice opened a box of mints, sat down on the bed, and began reading a ski magazine she had bought in the lobby. Eric carefully laid out her new nightgown on the bed.

There was a knock at the door. Eric opened it.

"I bet you don't remember who I am, do you," said a bald man whose stomach rolled over his wide western belt.

Eric looked at the grinning face. There was nothing familiar about it.

"Would it help if I told you my first name was Chuck?"

"Oh sure! Hi there, Chuck!" Eric was faking it.

"I bet you don't remember my last name, do you."

"Gee, it's on the tip of my tongue, Chuck."

"Willard—Chuck Willard. We had shop together in the eighth grade. Remember?"

Eric could not even remember taking shop in the eighth grade.

"Oh sure, it's all coming back to me now, Chuck."

"I knew it would," Chuck beamed. "Say, I was wondering if we could borrow a couple of chairs tonight. We've asked a few friends over to our room—you're not expecting company tonight, are you?"

"No, you go ahead, Chuck."

Chuck walked into the room. Janice grabbed the nightgown and stuffed it under the pillow.

"I remember you," Chuck said. "You're Martha Wilson. You played the accordion, right?"

"No, I'm sorry. I didn't even go to your high school."

"You're kidding! You're not Martha Wilson?"

"Sorry."

Chuck turned to Eric. "Doesn't she look like Martha Wilson?"

"I don't remember Martha, Chuck."

"You know, the one who played the accordion."

"Would you like some Girl Scout cookies?" Janice asked.

"Thanks," Chuck said, filling his sports coat pocket with half a box. "I'll just take a few now and eat them later. I can't eat sweets at night. It's a special diet. No sweets after supper. I just save 'em for morning. At first it seemed strange eating ice cream for breakfast, but I've gotten used to it."

Chuck grabbed the only two chairs in the room and left.

Janice started to read her magazine and eat cookies.

"You won't get crumbs in bed, will you?" Eric asked. "You know how I hate that."

"I'll be careful, dear."

"Crumbs in bed have always meant disorder and low life to me," he announced.

"I'm being very careful."

He paced the floor like a caged animal.

"There's no TV," he said.

"No, dear."

"Maybe we should go to bed," he suggested.

"I'm not very tired yet," she said, still reading.

He handed her the nightgown.

She stood up, looked at him seriously, and said, "Eric, there's something I need to talk to you about. It's very important to me."

"Yes?"

"How much do you know about the *H.M.S. Pinafore?*"

There was a knock at the door. "Anyone there?"

Eric opened the door.

"Surprise!" the couple at the door yelled.

Eric didn't recognize either of them. The man was tall and muscular with a deep tan. He wore cowboy boots and a western suit. The woman had blue eyes, a patch of freckles, and short, bouncy red hair.

"I bet you didn't expect to see us tonight, did you," she said energetically.

"Boy, I sure didn't."

"It's Bishop Turner now, isn't it?" the man asked, shaking hands. "We read about you in the book they gave us when we registered."

"Yes—won't you come in?"

As they turned to walk in, Janice was shoving the nightgown under the pillow.

She turned and smiled. "How nice of you to drop by."

They looked at the patch of nightgown still sticking from the pillow.

"First of all, do you know who we are?" the man asked.

Eric blanked out. "Let's see," he said, turning to the woman, "did you play the accordion?"

"I'm Ryan Carpenter and this is my wife Michelle."

"The football player Ryan Carpenter?" Eric asked.

Ryan smiled. "I'm flattered you remember. It's been twenty years now. Michelle was the homecoming queen her sophomore year, and she was a cheerleader too."

Eric looked at her again. Gradually the years peeled away and he was looking at a girl in a pom-pom outfit.

"I remember now."

"Do you remember something else?" she asked. "Ryan and I had to get married his senior year. It was the town scandal in 1961."

Eric remembered standing at his locker, overhearing the conversation of some fellows.

"She is, I tell you. Her stomach's blown up like a watermelon. Hey, here she comes now! See for yourself."

A girl, walking alone, her eyes straight ahead, approached them. Everyone turned to watch her pass, their eyes straining to see the bulge in her stomach.

"I can see it," one of the guys said.

"Gimme a P!" someone yelled.

"P!" the rest shouted.

"Gimme an R!"

And so forth through the word.

"What does it spell?"

"PREGNANT!" they all shouted.

"I CAN'T HEAR YOU!"

"PREGNANT!"

A teacher came by and told them to be quiet. The girl continued down the hall.

That was twenty years ago.

"I remember," Eric said.

Ryan put an arm around his wife's shoulder. "Our parents made us get married. I would have left right after the baby was born, except the Mormon missionaries came to our door. They taught Michelle first and she was baptized, and then I joined."

"The Church saved our marriage," she said. "So when we heard about the reunion, we decided to come. We want to tell the class of '61 how much the Church has meant in our lives. Our missionary son keeps sending us letters challenging us to do some missionary work. We wanted to get together with you and plan our missionary efforts. Bishop, what plans do you have for this weekend?"

Janice smiled. "She means as far as missionary work goes, dear."

Eric looked at Michelle's enthusiastic expression and decided she must generate two hundred watts of power just in her face.

"I want 'em to know what the Church has meant in our life," Michelle said. "But how can we do it?"

"Let's sleep on it and talk in the morning," Eric suggested.

While Janice and Michelle chatted about children, Ryan talked about his life. He had started as a carpenter, gone into real estate in Colorado, made some big investments in housing developments, made a lot of money, and recently bought himself a large ranch in Wyoming just for fun.

Eric asked him what he did in the Church.

He had served as an elders quorum president for several years, but a few months ago he had been called as a seventy. He spent most of his time working with part-member families, especially those with inactive or non-member husbands.

While Janice and Michelle continued visiting and Ryan went to get them some root beer, Eric stared at the mountain peak.

Sometimes he imagined he could transport himself to places just by thinking.

He stood on top of the peak, the icy winds blowing past his parka hood, gently moving his long beard. He stood on the veranda of his solar house built into the side of the cliff on top of the mountain. In the winter he sat in his studio and sculptured. In a few days an agent from the Metropolitan Museum of Art in New York City would come and buy his latest masterpiece.

" . . . didn't teethe until she was two years old," Janice was saying.

Ryan returned and said the machine was out of order. "Michelle," he said gently, "we should go now."

"Okay. Bishop, could we have a prayer with you and your wife before we leave?"

"What are we praying for?"

"That we'll have success in our missionary efforts this weekend."

He offered a brief prayer about setting good examples.

They left.

While Janice took a shower, he made a list of phone calls that still needed to be made. The only phone on the floor was in the hall. He used the ward's telephone credit card to phone his first counselor.

"Don, do you know if our bees have had Terramycin this spring?"

"No, but we'll find out tomorrow. The state bee inspector hit town today and wants to inspect our hives."

Eric returned to the room. The overhead light was not romantic. He draped his shirt over the reading light. It was much better that way.

Janice opened the door timidly, wearing the new nightgown.

"Don't look, Eric. It's awful. It's like hanging a curtain over the Goodyear blimp."

He switched off the reading light, and they stood by the window and kissed in the moonlight.

"The gerbil!" she gasped.

"What?"

"Oh, how could we? We left the gerbil alone in the house with nobody to feed it. Brent kept reminding us about it. Eric, it'd break his heart to lose his gerbil."

"What do you want me to do about it at this time of night? I'm sure it can wait till morning."

"We've got to do something. It's our only gerbil."

"Janice, I don't care about the gerbil. I never have. I care about us tonight—together—now."

"Well, I can't do anything until I'm absolutely sure the gerbil is taken care of."

Eric stormed away and flipped on both lights. She fell to her knees to avoid being seen through the window, started to crawl to the suitcase to get some clothes, then headed for the bathroom.

"Janice, it's almost midnight. There's nothing we can do tonight."

She paused on her hands and knees, then answered, "We'll call our home teachers."

"At midnight? You can't be serious. You want to call about a gerbil?"

She stepped into the bathroom and closed the door.

He talked to her through the door. "You're talking about a seventy-year-old man who's already had one heart attack. He goes to bed at eight-thirty."

"Then he's had four hours sleep. He'll be rested up."

She opened the door and was wearing a robe over the nightgown.

"I'm not letting you use the ward credit card for a gerbil," he flatly announced.

"Then please get me some change."

He got dressed.

They marched to the hall phone. She was barefoot,

and a trace of pink lace hung below her robe, but it seemed all right, because the hall was deserted. He went to get change while she waited by the phone.

The desk clerk was busy with someone else, so Eric waited. A large crowd had overflowed from the bar into the lobby. As far as the eye could see, people were slapping each other on the back and offering to buy the other a drink.

"Eric!"

He turned to face Ann. Over the years her figure had taken on the approximate shape of a grape, but her face still had some of the same youthful innocence and appeal.

"Ann! It's great to see you again."

"This is my husband, C.J."

They shook hands. C.J. looked like a mannequin from a clothing store. He and Ann both had drinks in their hands.

"It's 7-Up," she said, reading his mind. "C.J. is in the state senate race, and we thought if we mixed with people tonight, he could let 'em know about his campaign. Isn't that right, C.J.?"

He has a face for winning elections, Eric thought—thin, almost gaunt, with a full head of light brown hair.

"Always hard to knock off an incumbent, you know."

"C.J., tell him about your meeting with the governor last week."

C.J. smiled. "He doesn't want to know about that. Besides, I want to know more about the guy who nearly married my wife. What line of work are you in?"

Eric smiled but didn't say anything.

"Eric has a Ph.D.," Ann said. "My parents wrote me about it. I was so proud."

"What in?" C.J. asked.

"Physics."

"So you're probably doing some kind of research or teaching—right?"

"Not exactly," Eric stalled. "What do you do?"

"Several things actually—none of them very well."

They all grinned.

"Let's see—I'm on the board of directors of our hospital. I manage a clothing store, and sometimes I call myself an image analyst. Do you know what that is?"

Eric shook his head.

"People come to me to help 'em select their clothes on the basis of personality and career aspirations. Let's take you, for example. I presume you're doing research for some company or teaching in a university. Well, there's a certain type of image you want to convey . . . "

Eric had to tell them the truth. "Actually I've gone into business for myself."

"As a research consultant? I can tell you what kind of clothes will enhance your career aspirations."

"I run Lawn Doctor and manage an Orange Julius stand."

Nobody said anything for a few seconds.

"Oh," Ann finally stammered, "well, I bet your science background really comes in useful, doesn't it? I mean . . . precisely mixing the ingredients for an Orange Julius . . . " Her voice trailed off.

"You see," Eric explained, "after I got my Ph.D., there were a few years where it was hard to get jobs, so eventually I fell into this."

"Lawn Doctor," C.J. said. "I think we have a new franchise in our town. Let's see, you come out and mow the lawns, don't you?"

"We fertilize five times a year and spray for weeds and insects. We don't mow."

"It really sounds like a good deal, doesn't it, Ann?"

"Oh, yes," she said, a little too brightly. "Just look how tan he is."

There was silence for a moment.

"Is your wife here?" Ann finally said.

"Oh, my wife, I forgot about her. She's upstairs in the hall waiting for me to get change so we can use the phone."

"I'd really like to meet her," Ann said.

"You don't need change to phone long distance," C.J. suggested. "Just dial zero, the area code and the number you want, and you can charge it to your home phone."

As they reached the second-floor level and started down the hall, Eric could see an inch of nightgown showing below Janice's robe.

"Janice, here are some people I'd like you to meet. This is Ann, and her husband, C.J."

"Your Ann?" she asked.

They all chuckled in unison.

"You keep her barefoot like this all year?" C.J. joked.

Janice blushed. "I'm sorry for looking like this."

"Look, don't ever apologize for being pregnant," C.J. said. "Pregnancy is an important part of life."

"Well, I didn't dream we'd meet anyone out here," Janice said. "We have to make an emergency phone call."

"Nothing serious, I hope," Ann said.

"Just our gerbil. We left it all alone in the house with nobody to feed it."

Ann nodded sympathetically. "I know, I know. It's like one of your children, right? You go right ahead and phone."

C.J. had a puzzled expression on his face. "Is it trained to answer?"

Eric looked at him, decided he was serious, and didn't laugh.

"We're calling a friend to take care of it for the weekend," Janice said.

"Oh, sure."

Janice dialed the number.

After twenty rings, Brother Miller, their home teacher, answered it.

"Brother Miller, this is Janice Turner. You home teach us . . . No, Eric hasn't died . . . No, the house hasn't burned down . . . Well, yes, it is important. You see, we're away for the weekend and we left our gerbil all alone in the house . . . G-e-r-b-i-l. It's like a small rat . . . No, we don't want you to kill it. It's a pet. Could you get it and take it to your house and feed it till we get back? . . . No, it's in a cage . . . I'm sure it won't get out. Let me tell you where it is . . ."

C.J. opened a fresh roll of antacid tablets and put two in his mouth.

A few minutes later she was finished.

"Why don't you come to our room and we'll talk," Janice offered. "I have some nice cookies and mints."

"I think it's too late for that," Eric said, hoping to retrieve the night. "We all need to go to sleep."

They agreed to get together in the morning.

A few minutes later, Eric again waited for Janice to come out of the bathroom. He draped his shirt over the lamp again, then sat on the bed and stared at the mountain and transported himself to its top.

Janice and he stood in white fur robes in the comfort of their solar house built into the side of a cliff on the icy mountain peak. The light from a small fire played shadow games on their white fur rug and giant waterbed. She snuggled next to him—she was slim again. Outside just beyond the window stood the life-size ice sculpture he had done of her. It was pure and smooth and clear with no cracks and bubbles anywhere within the ice. Tomorrow a man from the Metropolitan Museum of Art would climb the vertical ice cliffs to offer him a fortune for his creation.

The knock at the door brought him off the mountain.

Eric didn't move.

"Bishop Turner?" a voice called out. "Are you awake?"

Janice, still in her nightgown, sat down on the bed beside him and touched his hand.

"Oh, Janice," he moaned. "I'm so tired."

"I know, dear."

"Why can't we ever have time to ourselves?"

She touched his face. "Because you're a wonderful man, that's why. It's probably nothing. I'll just slip into the bathroom again, and you answer it."

He got up and pulled his shirt and slacks on again, then opened the door.

It was Dale Warren and his girl friend, Noelle.

"Bishop, we need to talk to you," Dale said.

Oh, no, Eric thought. *There goes his mission.*

Once inside they looked around for some chairs.

"Go ahead and sit on the bed."

They sat down.

"Is anything wrong?" Eric asked.

"I've decided I don't want to go on a mission. I want to marry Noelle."

"Are you still worthy to go on a mission?" he asked.

"Yes. We haven't done anything wrong."

"Then what's the problem?"

"We love each other, bishop," Noelle said.

"I don't know what I'd do if Noelle married someone else while I was gone. I don't want to take that chance."

Janice came out wearing slacks and a blouse.

"Why, Dale and Noelle! What a nice surprise! You came all this way just to visit us? Let me get you some cookies and mints."

They sampled the mints.

"Janice, I need to talk to Dale and Noelle alone for a while."

"No problem, I'll just go back into the bathroom and brush my teeth." She took a few mints in with her.

They could hear loud singing from the bar downstairs.

"Is it wrong to be so much in love that we don't want to be apart?" Noelle asked.

"No, that's not wrong."

"But you think I should serve my mission first, right?" Dale asked.

Eric had them move apart so he could sit between them.

"Dale, how much do you love Noelle?"

"More than anything in the world."

"Then don't marry her now—wait two years."

"We don't want to wait," Dale said.

"Noelle, have you ever thought about going to college? Have you ever wanted to save up some money and take off for Hawaii? Do you ever dream of touring through Europe? Or learning to fly an airplane? Or owning a sports car? Or gaining professional skills? Do you ever dream about things like that?"

"I don't care about any of that now, bishop."

"But someday you might."

"How do you know?"

He smiled. "Because I'm a thousand years old."

"What do you mean?" she asked.

"Since I've been a bishop, many people have come to me with their problems. I've gone through the equivalent of hundreds of years of life talking to them. Let me tell you about a composite of some of these people. She's twenty-four years old, married for the past six or seven years. She has two children. She got married just out of high school. Her husband never had a chance to learn a trade, and so in order to make ends meet, he has two jobs. She babysits part-time.

"One day while she's changing a diaper, she decides she's had it. She wants to be free to travel or to go to college or take a full-time job. She's tired of playing house.

"She comes and tells me she want to *live*. She wants to be *free*. Maybe she talks about divorce. She says she doesn't love her husband anymore.

"What can I tell her? I can't encourage her to get a divorce. You can't walk out of a marriage just because you want to be eighteen and single again.

"Dale, let this girl have some time to spend on herself. Let her develop her talents. Let her become a woman before you marry her."

Next he turned to Noelle.

"Let him go on a mission. The next two years isn't your time—it's the Lord's time. When Dale comes back from his mission, he'll have the maturity of a man ten years older. He'll have confidence in prayer; he'll know how to set goals; he'll have a testimony. Together, with both of you much stronger, you can have a wonderful life together—both strong, both equally yoked, both dedicated to the Lord and to each other."

They were both silent until Noelle said quietly, "Dale, maybe he's right."

"But what if you don't wait for me?" Dale asked.

"I will."

"But what if you don't?"

"Then you'll have to marry someone else. Bishop, did you have a girl waiting for you on your mission?"

"Yes."

"Did she wait for you the whole time?"

"No, she got married."

"See what I mean?" Dale said.

"But God isn't going to make you worse off in your marriage because you serve on a mission. How could I ever have done better than my wife?"

They could hear Janice energetically brushing her teeth.

Someone ran down the hall yelling, "The British are coming!"

Eric walked to the bathroom door and let Janice know she could come out.

"Well, I certainly have sparkling teeth now," she bubbled.

Dale stood and shook Eric's hand. "Okay, I'll go on my mission, bishop. We'd better go home now."

"It's too late," Eric said. "Stay until morning."

"I guess we could sleep in the car," Dale said.

"Let's figure out something better than that," Eric suggested.

They decided that Janice and Noelle would sleep on the bed while Dale and Eric slept on the floor. Eric phoned the parents to explain everything, then they had prayers, and with everyone still in their clothes, they turned off the lights to go to sleep.

Five minutes later, Dale complained, "Bishop, it's no use. I can't sleep in the same room with Noelle."

"Why not?"

"I can hear her breathing," he said. Eric turned on the light. It was one-thirty in the morning.

"Come with me then."

Eric and Dale went downstairs. With the closing of the bar, it was now quiet. They went into the large lounge area with the fireplace and each picked a sofa.

"Bishop?" Dale said as they both looked at the mountain peak.

"Yes."

"I knew you'd be able to help us."

CHAPTER FOUR

The desert wind howled around him. On the next ridge he could just make out the outlines of an oasis. He fell down, crawled painfully toward the green trees.

He was very close to the oasis, but the wind was growing louder.

"Okay, fella, the party's over. Time to sober up." He opened his eyes. The cleaning lady stood over him. She turned off the vacuum cleaner. The howling stopped.

He sat up and looked at his watch. It was six-thirty.

"You must have had some night," she said.

She went to the next sofa and woke Dale.

It was too early to wake up Janice and Noelle, so they went for a walk.

"Bishop, when you were in high school, did you dream of being Lawn Doctor?"

Eric shook his head. "It just worked out that way."

An hour later they went upstairs and woke up Janice and Noelle. Dale was anxious to leave, and so they took two boxes of mints and left.

When Eric and Janice entered the dining area, they saw C.J. walking around shaking hands and passing out pamphlets for his state senate bid. Eric and Janice got their food and sat down. Five minutes later C.J. and Ann joined them.

"Did you see our car in the parking lot?" C.J. asked. "Brand new—we picked it up yesterday."

"How do you like it?" Janice asked.

"Fine. You know, it's hard to pick a car when you're in

the public eye. A man's car is part of his image. I couldn't get a Cadillac, because people'd figure I was crooked. Ann was showing me an article the other day about how much corruption there is in politics. It showed a mayor standing in front of his Cadillac.

"But on the other hand, you can't get a Ford either, because then people won't respect you. So it's somewhere between those two. You have to look successful—but not too successful. We finally decided on a Buick diesel. I think it's going to work out—imagewise. Of course, the whole thing is tax deductible. Otherwise who can afford anything?"

"Sure," Eric said dully.

"What kind of car do you drive?" C.J. asked.

"A '70 Coronet station wagon."

"Oh . . . well . . . I guess that's all you need . . . I mean, for your line of work."

A few minutes later the conversation drifted to church.

"C.J." Ann said, "tell them the story you gave in your talk last Sunday."

C.J. finished a mouthful before talking. "When Ann and I were first married, we lived in this small apartment. One day the bathroom drain wouldn't work. We used drain cleaner, but it didn't do any good. Finally we called up the landlord. When he came, he undid the trap below the drain and found a plastic cap. We could have poured drain cleaner down there all day and it wouldn't have done any good. Well, I asked the landlord why he hadn't poured drain cleaner down the drain, and he said—and this is something I've never forgotten—he said, 'No use doing that till you first see what's plugging it up.' "

Eric and Janice looked blankly at C.J.

"Well, I got to thinking. Isn't that just like life? How many of us in the Drain Pipe of Life don't first find out what's plugging us up?" His voice trailed off as he saw the look on Eric's face.

"Well," Janice said kindly after several seconds of silence. "I don't think I've ever heard that story before in a talk."

"Eric," Ann said, "what are you doing in the Church these days?"

"I'm a bishop."

A cloud passed over C.J.'s face, then disappeared. Eric had seen the look before, the look of someone feeling guilty about talking to a bishop, someone with something to hide.

"I'm proud of you," Ann said.

C.J. took two pills after breakfast. "They're for my ulcer," he explained.

Ann talked about gardening. "Did you know that radishes planted near cabbage repel maggots?"

Neither Eric nor Janice knew that.

C.J. left to phone about his campaign.

"Eric," Ann said, "there's a question I've always wanted to ask you. It's a science question. I know you have all that training in science, and I'll bet you could answer it."

"I'll try."

"You know in the story of Goldilocks and the Three Bears, when Mama Bear dished out the porridge it was too hot so they went for a walk to let it cool off. Well, when Goldilocks tasted it later, she found Papa Bear's was too hot, Mama Bear's too cold, but Baby Bear's was just right. It always seems strange that Mama Bear's was too cold, because the smaller portion should cool off faster, shouldn't it? I think Baby Bear's porridge should have been the coldest. Why is it the way it says in the story?"

"I've never thought about it much before."

"Oh—I thought, with all your schooling . . . Well, I guess it was a dumb question after all, wasn't it."

He decided to give it a try. "Maybe Mama Bear's bowl was made out of a different material—like aluminum. That would conduct heat away faster and cool off quicker."

"I bet that's it," Ann said.

From there the conversation between Janice and Ann drifted to making fruit leather.

Eric stared out the window and looked at the mountain peak again.

He stood in his living room overlooking the world, taking one last look at his ice sculpture. It would be his last day with it. Far below, the man from the Metropolitan Museum of Art painfully inched his way up the vertical ice wall. He would be there in another hour.

Suddenly a helicopter cleared the windswept ridge and lowered a man down on the cable. The name painted on the helicopter read "Guggenheim Museum."

Everyone wanted his ice sculpture, his one lasting contribution to the world.

Back in the dining room, with his mind still on the mountain, he was drinking his grape juice when someone walked by the table and slapped him on the shoulder. Eric spilled the juice all over his shirt.

"Great seeing you here!" the unidentified class member said as he moved on.

Eric looked down at the grape stain on his shirt.

"To remove a stain like that," Ann said enthusiastically, "all you have to do is stretch the stained area over a bowl, stand up on a ladder, and pour boiling water over it."

"That's nice to know," Janice said.

"But the most important thing is to do something within the first five minutes. That's the most crucial time for a stain. C'mon, Eric, we'll go to the kitchen, get some boiling water, and find a ladder."

"Is the ladder really all that important?" Janice asked skeptically.

"I usually do it with a ladder," Ann said. "C'mon, Eric."

"You don't need to bother," Janice said with just the hint of an edge to her voice. "I know how to remove stains too, you know."

"Do you use a ladder?" Ann asked.

"No, what I do is . . . "

A minute later Eric was escorted quickly to their room so he could give up his shirt. Then Janice and Ann hurried away to find a ladder.

Down in the lobby in a clean shirt a few minutes later, he saw Ryan and Michelle distributing pamphlets.

"We're done!" Michelle announced proudly. "We've scattered pamphlets all over the place."

"Humor her," Ryan said, smiling. "She's been embarrassing me all day. She made me go into the sauna and leave pamphlets. That wouldn't have been too bad, but it was during women's hours."

"Well," she said, "at least you got their attention. But guess what, bishop. Last night we thought of having a little Sunday church service and inviting our whole class to it. Then we'll have a chance to tell everyone about the Church. Be sure and tell everyone you see today about it, okay?"

Eric was sure it wouldn't work. "Sometimes things don't always work out the way we'd like them to," he commented.

She laughed. "And sometimes they do."

Ryan looked at the clock. "We'd better hurry. The schedule says there's a softball game starting in fifteen minutes. C'mon, bishop."

Ryan was chosen for one side, Eric the other.

The team captain for Eric's team was Horse McCracken. He and Ryan had been the school's sports heroes. Horse had played college football, then pro ball, before settling down and managing a car dealership in Pomona. Since high school, he had put on a lot of weight, but his voice was still the same—loud and raunchy.

The first time at bat, Ryan hit a home run. As he trotted around the bases, he stopped at each base and gave out a pamphlet and an invitation to the Sunday meeting.

Michelle ran out and hugged him when he finally crossed home plate—not so much for the home run as for giving out the pamphlets.

The next batter hit a long fly ball to Eric in left field. He misjudged and it bounced past him.

"Wake up out there!" Horse growled.

For the next few minutes nothing happened in left field. That gave Eric a chance to look at the mountain.

He stood in front of his ice sculpture talking to Barbara Walters on nationwide TV.

"Eric," Barbara said, "I'm sure you were saddened as we all were with the fall of Lars Degman of the Metropolitan Museum of Art just a few minutes ago."

"Yes I was, Barbara. If I'd known he was in trouble, I'd have rappelled down and rescued him."

Barbara looked sadly into the camera. "Too bad for Lars and too bad for the Metropolitan Museum. I understand now that you've decided to let the Guggenheim Museum have your ice sculpture."

"That's right, Barbara. They have a helicopter, you know."

"Eric, let me ask you a question. Why do you spend your life up here on this mountain sculpturing?"

He looked into the camera. "I guess it's my way of leaving the world a better place."

"Critics describe your work as pure genius. How does that make you feel?"

"Humble, I'd say, Barbara. May I call you Barb?"

"Barb?" she asked, raising her eyebrows.

"Yes. It does, it makes me humble."

She reached over and touched him on the arm. "Eric, do you think of yourself as a genius?"

He looked into the camera, paused, and said sincerely, "Yes, I do, Barb."

"YOU STUPID IDIOT! WHO EVER TOLD YOU YOU COULD PLAY BALL? CATCH THE BALL WHEN IT COMES TO YOU—DON'T JUST LOOK AT WHERE IT BOUNCES! YOU NUMSKULL!"

Ryan had just hit an in-the-park home run, thanks to Eric missing the ball. Three people scored.

Eventually, no thanks to Eric, the inning ended.

When Eric returned to the bench, Horse chewed him out again.

"Hey, take it easy," Eric objected. "After all, it's just a friendly game."

Horse grabbed his shoulder. "Listen to me! Of course it's a friendly game, but we're going to blow 'em off the field. If there's one thing I've learned in life it's this—be pleasant but go for the jugular. Remember that!"

Ryan was the pitcher. Just before starting, he walked over to Eric. "You're just sitting alone. Go and talk with some of the guys."

Eric shook his head. "Ryan, they're all telling dirty jokes, just like they did in high school. In fact, they're the same jokes."

"C'mon, at least talk to somebody and tell 'em about the meeting tomorrow."

Eric sighed, then walked over and sat down by a man he vaguely remembered who was nursing a six-pack of beer.

"Great being together here again, huh?" Eric said.

"Sure."

"You know," Eric said, "I was reading in *Sports Illustrated* the other day that over thirty million people play amateur softball in this country. Amazing, isn't it?"

"Sure. Have a beer?"

"No thanks. Let's see—I can't remember your name."

"Bucky Barnes."

"Oh sure. I'm Eric Turner."

"I thought so. Seeing you out there in left field making a fool of yourself brought back old memories. We used to have gym together."

Bucky took a long drink and wiped his chin with his sleeve.

"You know, Turner, I never really liked you in high school. Actually I guess it'd be more honest to say I hated your guts—but no hard feelings now, okay?"

"Okay, Bucky."

"Sure you don't want a beer?"

Eric looked desperately at the mountain but couldn't get himself up there.

"You want to know why I hated your guts?"

"Not really."

"It was because you never shared your algebra homework with any of us. Always had to be the big genius, didn't you? Go ahead, smart guy, tell me what you're doing these days. Running some research lab or teaching at some big university? Go ahead—I know you're dying to tell me."

"Bucky, you know, for a while there was a shortage of jobs in science. Of course it's a lot better now. In fact, there's a shortage of trained engineers and scientists who can work in industry, but a few years ago . . ."

"So what do you do?"

"I'm in business, Bucky. I manage two businesses."

"Yeah, what kind?"

"I manage a store in a new shopping mall."

"What is it, some kind of computer store?"

Eric mumbled, "Orange Julius."

"I didn't hear you."

"Orange Julius."

Bucky choked on his beer, spraying foam into the air. He slid off the bench laughing.

"What's the other business?" he asked as soon as he could get control of himself again.

"I'm Lawn Doctor."

Bucky was still howling as Eric walked to the batter's box.

I'll show them, he thought. *I'll show them all.*

Janice and Ann arrived in time to watch him bat. Ann waved the stain-free shirt at him.

He struck out, retiring the side.

The next inning was good. Nobody hit the ball to Eric. Just before his team batted again, a woman suddenly appeared at home plate and wouldn't budge.

"Why aren't there women playing here?" she demanded.

"Because baseball's a man's game!" Horse yelled. "Now get away from there before you get hurt!"

"I'm not moving till there's equal numbers of men and women on the teams. We don't have to take this discrimination anymore."

"I know you," Horse growled. "You're Kelli Grumbaugh. What's happened to you? You were a nice girl in high school."

She picked up a bat and started swinging it. "That was two dead-beat husbands, three dead-end secretary jobs, and twenty years ago. It's guys like you, with loud mouths and no brains and a few beers, that've made my life miserable. I'm not moving, Horse Face."

Horse strode to the pitcher's mound, took the ball from Ryan, and wound up. "Get out of the way, sister, or I'll knock you away!"

Kelli stepped into the batter's box. "Go ahead and try, Bozo."

"You'll think Bozo." Horse threw the ball. She knocked it out of the park.

He threw another ball, and she hit a line drive that nearly parted his hair. He had to dive for the ground to avoid being hit.

A minute later he got up, dusted himself off, spat, rearranged his hat, and asked, "Okay, whadaya want?"

"We choose up sides again. Five men and five women to a team."

There was a shortage of women. They talked Janice into playing, promising that all she had to do was to stand at third base and wait for someone to throw the ball to her. Eric was the last player chosen—even after Janice. He ended up sitting on the bench as a substitute.

In the first inning of the new game, Horse hit a hard line drive into right field. In trying to stretch it into a double, he purposely crashed into the second baseman.

As the injured player sat on the ground, dazed and groggy, blood dripped from his nose onto his shirt.

Ann trotted in from center field.

"I know a way," she announced to nobody in particular, "to get blood stains from clothing. You just cover the area with meat tenderizer and apply cool water to make a paste. Wait half an hour, then sponge with cool water."

Nobody seemed to care.

The game ended for lunch just after Janice hit a pop-up to the pitcher.

Eric and Janice started walking back to the lodge.

"Hi, Eric," the mysterious blonde called out on her way to go swimming in the motel pool across the way.

Eric's mouth dropped open as he looked at her in her swimming suit.

"Hi there," he croaked.

She walked with them.

"We still need to get together and talk about all the old times."

He felt Janice's laser eyes boring a hole through him.

"Oh sure," he said.

"See you around, honey."

"You don't know who she is," Janice said.

"No idea."

"Eric, it's all right if you have something to say. Maybe it was something you're ashamed to talk about, but it was a long time ago, and I'll understand."

"There's nothing at all. I would've remembered if there was, wouldn't I?"

Janice watched the blonde depart. "Yes, I think you would."

"I swear there was nothing. I don't know who she is."

"Hmmm," Janice said, unconvinced.

Kelli, the one who had stood up to Horse, caught up with them. She said how impressed she was with Janice for playing softball even though she was pregnant. She talked about the importance of raising the consciousness of women everywhere.

"You can do anything you want and be anything you want. What do you want?"

"I want to be a wife and mother."

"No, no—I mean *anything*. You could be a national leader."

Janice smiled. "Oh, not me."

"Why not? I'm talking anything. Think about it."

"You think so?" Janice asked.

Kelli left a few minutes later.

As Eric and Janice walked toward the lodge for lunch, she started to sing to herself, softly at first, but then more loudly.

CHAPTER FIVE

1961

Ryan lay in bed and waited, his eyes closed as if he were asleep.

Michelle padded into the room, knelt down by the side of the bed, and began her silent prayer.

He opened his eyes and stared at his wife of four months, now seven months pregnant.

Her face was softly lit by the neon sign of the store across the street from their second-floor apartment. She didn't say anything, but he could see her lips moving. Her face had never seemed more beautiful to him, free of the stress he put there each day by the way he treated her—when he ignored her for days at a time, when they didn't talk, when he tried to punish her for wrecking his life, for keeping him from a football career—for getting pregnant.

The day she told him was the day he quit caring about her. He was trapped in a marriage he never wanted. But it wouldn't last. As soon as she had the baby, he was leaving her.

In the meantime he punished her. Silence was the weapon. When he came home from work, he grumbled his way through supper, then left to work on his car or go drinking with friends.

He figured he was the one who earned the money, so he should decide how to spend it. He doled out a little to her each week, but made her ask, almost beg, for anything else.

But something was happening to ruin his fun.

Six weeks earlier when he came home from work, she told him that two Mormon missionaries had come during the day and talked to her. They wanted to return and teach them both.

"Not me," he said.

"I want to hear what they have to say."

"Suit yourself. I don't care what you do."

They came. He made sure he wasn't home.

The days slipped by. Pamphlets began to fill their magazine rack.

In a way it was better that she was being taught. That gave him an excuse to stay away.

One night when he came home she was waiting up.

"I want to get baptized."

"I don't care what you do."

"They said I should talk to you. They said you're the head of our family."

"Let's get one thing straight," he snapped. "We don't have a family. The only reason I married you was because your dad said he'd send me to jail if I didn't. So I did, but I didn't want to. And as soon as you have the kid, I'm leaving. So don't start on me about 'our family.' You do whatever you want—whatever you'd do if I weren't here, because before very long I won't be."

In a way he wanted to see her crawl, to beg him to stay, to offer to quit meeting with the Mormons. But there was something in her face, something he'd never seen before in anyone. He didn't like it.

"I'll be baptized on Saturday—if you want to watch."

He made a point to get drunk Friday night. He went to work Saturday morning, but started drinking again in the afternoon. By late afternoon, he was very drunk. He staggered in and fell on the bed.

He woke up at ten o'clock at night, went to the bathroom, returned, pulled off his jeans and shirt, purposely dropped them on the floor for her to pick up, then crawled under the covers.

A few minutes later, she came into the room. He closed his eyes.

At first he thought she had lost something on the floor. Then he opened his eyes and saw her on her knees praying by the bed.

He wasn't sure why watching her pray made such an impression on him. Religion was not something he'd had in his home when he grew up. His feelings about God alternated between thinking of Him as a stern ruler who'd zap you if you crossed Him up, and thinking of Him as a fairy tale.

He looked at her and suddenly realized what fascinated him so much.

She wasn't afraid—and he was. He was afraid of God. God was going to get him for getting her pregnant.

Something had happened a few days after rumors about Michelle's being pregnant floated through the school. A girl, her face without makeup of any kind, her manner austere, had come up to him in the halls where he had spent the day smirking with the guys who kidded him about Michelle. "You can't mock God," she had said sternly. "God will punish you for your sin."

He laughed about it to others, but deep inside he had taken it as a sign.

So he had been waiting for God to get him. Maybe it would be leprosy or something worse. Or maybe he'd crash his car. What would it be? Sometimes he thought about what he'd do if he were God and somebody crossed him. That made him scared.

She isn't afraid of God, he thought. *Why isn't she afraid?*

The next night he left a winning poker game to go home early enough to watch her pray.

That week he watched her three times.

Friday after work he attended a kegger with some friends. They sat by the bank of a river and drank.

"What's your name again?" he asked the girl next to him as they drank and tossed pebbles into the river.

"Pat," she said.

"Yeah, Pat. Do you ever pray?"

She laughed.

"I mean it. Close your eyes and let me see you pray."

She swore at him.

He reached over to push her head down, but she squirmed away and stood up.

He followed her.

"Get away," she warned.

"I just want to see you pray. Close your eyes and fold your arms."

He touched her shoulder and she screamed. Someone came behind him and hit him on the head. He passed out.

When he awoke, it was late at night. Everyone had gone. He was lying in the back seat of his car.

He looked at the stars. Thousands of them filled the night sky.

He had forgotten about stars.

If God was out to get us, why did he go to the trouble of making the night sky look so good? He didn't need to go to all that work if sooner or later all he was going to do was to zap us anyway.

Maybe God isn't out to destroy us, he thought. *Maybe all he's trying to do is keep us from destroying ourselves.*

He crawled to the front seat and turned on the radio and listened. It wasn't until sunrise that he felt good enough to drive home.

He stood for a few minutes in the doorway of their bedroom, looking at Michelle. Shafts of sunlight made golden patterns across the bed. He sat down and watched her sleep. Her bulging stomach almost made a tent of the covers.

It was the first time since they'd been married that he realized he loved her.

"Michelle," he whispered.

She opened her eyes. "What's wrong?"

"Nothing. I want to watch you pray. I've seen you before."

She sat up. "Why do you watch me pray?"

"I don't know why. Please."

She knelt down beside the bed and bowed her head, then looked at him. "I feel strange knowing you're watching. Why don't we pray together?"

He nodded and knelt down beside her.

She started to cry. He tenderly wiped away her tears.

"I didn't know if you'd come back," she said.

She prayed, and he opened his eyes to see her face. For one golden moment it seemed that was the closest he would ever be to God.

They lay in bed and he held her hand, but soon fell asleep.

At seven-thirty, she got him up so he could go to work.

He was curious about something she had said in her prayer. He asked during breakfast. "Who was Joseph Smith?"

"He was a prophet."

"What does that mean?"

"God talks to a prophet—like Moses."

She timidly asked after a long silence, "Do you want to know more?"

"Is it the reason you pray?"

"Yes."

"I guess I do then."

They ate breakfast without much talk, both embarrassed at feeling so close to each other.

"I'm going to a lumberyard this morning after work," he said.

"Oh?"

"To get some wood. I'm going to make a cradle for our baby."

The tears ran down their cheeks, but neither one mentioned it to the other.

That morning he bought the wood, and he never left her alone again.

After the baby was born, Ryan worked construction as a carpenter. They moved from town to town wherever the work led. He worked on apartment buildings and shopping malls and whatever could keep him busy for a few months. They bought a small trailer to live in.

The money was good when he was working. But in the winter there was no work.

During the second year of their marriage, times were hard. He worked on one job, but then his boss went broke and couldn't pay him. All he got out of the deal was a broken-down dump truck.

Their pick-up needed a new transmission and he was out of work. They were down to noodles and tomato soup.

He heard about construction in Colorado. They threw some things into the cab of the truck and headed for Denver.

Still seventy miles from Denver, they spent their last dollar on gas for the truck. It was late at night in September.

Twenty miles later the headlights went out.

Ryan drove in the dark until he was stopped by the highway patrol and told he couldn't go until he had headlights.

They sat in the dark. Ryan got out, opened the hood, and turned on the flashlight, but it was out of batteries. With silent fury, he flung the flashlight as far as he could.

Their baby, Danny, was crying. Michelle started to nurse him. Ryan opened the nearly empty sack of food and gave her the last sandwich and the last of the milk.

"What about you?" she asked.

"I'm not hungry," he lied.

He sat and listened to Danny nurse and watched the cars whiz past them in the night.

A cold wind started to blow.

"What are we going to do?" she asked.

He shook his head. "We're out of money. You and

Danny shouldn't be here. You'd better go home to your parents till I get work."

She held the baby up to her shoulder and patted him so he'd burp. "I'm not leaving you."

"There's no more food."

"I'm not leaving you, not ever. You'll figure out something."

In frustration he slammed his fist into the door. The noise started their son crying.

Michelle began to nurse him again.

"Well, I think we should pray," she said.

"What good will that do?"

She looked at him. "You know it'll help."

"Will you say the prayer?"

"I think you should."

"Why?"

"You know more about what we need than I do."

He nodded and closed his eyes. "God," he said, "this is no place for my wife and baby. Get us out of here. Amen."

A few minutes later, a trucker stopped to help. Ryan explained the problem.

"Just a minute," the trucker said. He took out a stick of gum from his pocket. "This'll fix you up."

He put the gum in his mouth and started chewing, then carefully separated the aluminum backing from the paper and wrapped the aluminum foil around the bad fuse. Ryan turned on the lights. They worked.

"An old trucker's trick," he said. "Better than a penny, 'cause if you get pushing too many amps through the foil, the foil will melt."

A minute later they were on their way.

They arrived in Denver two hours later. Ryan rolled out the sleeping bag and put it around them, and they waited for morning.

At seven o'clock he woke up. They were out of clean diapers and food. He woke Michelle up, and together they searched behind the seat for loose change and found seventy-eight cents. He walked half a block to a grocery store, where he bought a quart of milk and a loaf of discounted bread.

They ate the bread and milk.

"This is the last of our money," he said.

"I know."

"So maybe we ought to pray again," he suggested.

By nine that morning he had a job building a large apartment.

* * * * *

At first they planned to stay in Denver only while there was work at the apartment complex.

He was asked to home teach, even though he wasn't an elder yet.

One of the families he was assigned was the Robbins family, consisting of the wife, Angie, and three small children. Her husband, Kirk, was inactive in the Church.

The first time they called, Angie gathered all the children into the living room. At the same time Kirk escaped through the kitchen into the backyard.

"We're ready for your lesson," Angie said.

Ryan turned to his companion, a fifteen-year-old boy named Bruce.

"You teach the lesson," he said, abandoning the family as he followed Kirk outside.

"Me?" Bruce asked.

Ryan found Kirk in his garage working on his car. He rolled up his sleeves and helped.

An hour later the job was done. "Thanks," Kirk said, still off balance by this new home teacher.

"I'll be back in two weeks. Think of a project you need help on. I'm a carpenter by trade."

"No kidding," Kirk said.

The next time he went, they built a bookcase. Then to return the favor, Kirk invited Ryan fishing.

The next time they came, Kirk didn't leave the living room.

"I don't have a lesson. I thought we were going to work," Ryan said.

"You're supposed to give us a lesson," Angie said.

"Why?" Ryan asked.

"You're supposed to teach us so our children will know how to live."

"Kirk can do that. I'm just here to help him."

"Oh, you're wasting your time with him," Angie said. "He'll never get interested in the Church."

"If you were my wife," Ryan said, "I wouldn't either."

She blanched.

The next time they visited, he still didn't have a lesson.

"You never give us a lesson," Angie said.

"Okay, I have a lesson. The lesson is—quit treating your husband like dirt just because he doesn't go to church. He does a lot of good things, you know. He's a better man than you probably deserve."

He left to go to the garage with Kirk to learn how to tie flies.

The next Sunday, the bishop cornered him. "What are you doing with the Robbins family? I got two phone calls last week. The first from Sister Robbins demanding that I change home teachers, and the second one from Kirk demanding that I keep you."

The next time he visited, Angie was ready. She'd hidden a tape recorder so she could record what was said, to prove to the bishop what a lousy home teacher she had.

"We're ready for your lesson now," she said.

"I don't have a lesson."

"I knew you wouldn't."

The silence dragged on.

"Well, maybe we could just talk," Kirk said.

"About what?" Ryan asked.

"He's supposed to have a lesson," Angie said again.

"I bet you'd like me to get active in the Church and take my family to the temple, wouldn't you?" Kirk asked.

"Yeah, sure. Michelle and I'd go with you. We haven't gone either."

Angie turned to her husband. "You'll never change."

"Angie," Ryan said, "why don't you shut up for a minute so Kirk and I can talk."

"Of course," she said smugly, happy she was recording the conversation.

"The biggest problems I have are drinking and tithing," Kirk said. "The rest I think I could do."

"I used to drink," Ryan said. "What's your favorite brand of beer?"

"Coors," Kirk said.

"Not me. I like Olympia. I still remember the way a can felt in my hand on a hot day after work. Sometimes when I'm real thirsty, I miss it."

"But you gave it up, didn't you?" Kirk asked.

"Yeah."

"Why?"

"Why do you think?"

"Because you found something better?"

"That's it."

Kirk thought a minute. "I could give it up too."

Angie looked at him as if he were a stranger.

"Tithing'd be a problem though," Kirk said.

"For me too," Ryan admitted.

They sat and thought.

"I will if you will," Kirk finally agreed.

"Let me think about it for a couple of weeks," Ryan said.

The next Sunday the bishop asked to talk with Ryan in his office. He played the tape of Ryan's visit.

"Yeah, so what?" Ryan asked.

"Well, it's probably not a good idea to tell the wife to shut up while you're home teaching."

"She's a pain—she's the one stopping Kirk from going to church. Anything else you want to say, bishop?"

"If you pay tithing, I promise you the Lord will bless you financially and spiritually," he said.

Ryan started paying tithing.

The next time Ryan went home teaching, Kirk also made a commitment to pay tithing.

A month later Ryan was laid off from work.

The bishop, who had promised great blessings for paying tithing, broke out into a sweat every time he saw Ryan in church. Finally he called Ryan up. "I've got a job for you—selling real estate."

"I don't know anything about that."

"You can learn."

"I'm a carpenter."

"Look, you'll be good at it. How many other salesmen can answer questions about how a house is built? In time it'll pay more than you're making."

"Who'll I be working for?"

"Me."

Ryan took the job and started selling, just in time for a boom in population in Denver.

Six months later Ryan and Michelle and Kirk and Angie went through the temple.

Ryan and Michelle stayed in Denver and grew with it. Their bishop called him as his executive secretary mainly to have him attend some of the leadership meetings—because he had a talent for cutting through to the heart of the issue.

Like the time the elders quorum president was looking for a secretary.

The bishop went through the list one more time. "Don Pierce."

"He's inactive," the elders quorum president said.

Ryan shook his head and laughed. "Mormons are crazy."

"Why?"

"Because the Inactives are more active than the Actives. They go hunting and fishing and boating and skiing and build bookcases and work on their cars. And what do the Actives do? They sit in church and feel bad about not doing genealogy. I think the Inactives are the best part of this church, and I think the Actives ought to visit 'em just to learn something."

The bishop was grinning appreciatively.

"So how does that solve the problem of finding a secretary?" the elders quorum president asked.

"What's so hard about the job? Just ask anybody on the list. Tell 'em what you want 'em to do. And if they want to do it, they'll say yes."

"It won't work," the elders quorum president said.

Ryan picked up the list of inactive men and randomly placed his finger on one of the names. "Let me ask him if he'll do it."

They looked at the man's name. "He'll never do it, not in a million years."

Ryan visited the man, who accepted the assignment. Halfway through the first presidency meeting the man went outside for a smoke. But that only lasted a few months—while he prepared to take his wife through the temple.

Ryan went from being a carpenter to selling real estate to financing the building of duplex apartments. A few years later he was building large condominiums in the Denver area.

He served for ten years as an elders quorum president, until finally, just before the reunion, he and his wife were called to be stake missionaries.

Through all his church experience, he never learned the tragic phrase—"he'll never change."

CHAPTER SIX

1961-1963

By the end of his senior year, Eric wanted to serve a mission. He was also sure enough about his love for Ann to give her an engagement ring before he left.

* * * * *

He'd been on his mission for twenty months. His companion was Elder Leon Hart, who had been on his mission a year but still complained because he wasn't in another mission.

"In California, they don't go door-to-door tracting."

"We're not in California, elder."

"I don't like to go tracting."

"Me either. I would rather people called us up and asked to be baptized, but they don't, so we go tracting."

"Why don't we try inspiration tracting?"

"What's that?" Eric asked.

"You just drive until the Spirit whispers for you to stop."

The effort ended when they ran out of gas.

* * * * *

Eric never would forget the day he got his Dear John letter from Ann.

They had just arrived home for lunch. Hart was making fried bologna sandwiches and warm Jello to drink. Eric went to the mailbox and found a curiously thin letter from Ann. He read it on the way in.

"The past few weeks have been so wonderful . . . I've met someone very special. . . . Last night he asked me to marry him. . . . I know this will be a disappointment to you, but I know you will find someone else."

"Soup's on!" Hart announced. Elder Hart always said that, but they seldom had soup.

Eric sat down at the table, still stunned. After the blessing on the food, he just stared at his sandwich. Finally he opened it up and looked at the curled-up fried bologna. His life was now the way the bologna looked.

"I think we ought to paint the kitchen again," Hart said. "I have this certain shade in mind that'd really go with the linoleum." He stopped to look at Eric. "Not hungry today?"

"I just got a Dear John letter."

Hart laughed. "Too bad," he roared. "That's one thing'll never happen to me. My girl loves me."

Eric tried the warm Jello drink.

"Why do we always have this slop for lunch?" he asked.

"I like it." Hart pulled out a wallet and showed Eric a picture of his girl. "Pretty, huh?"

"She's okay."

"Okay? Is that all you can say? Look at her face and that hair. It's almost strawberry blonde. If we go to a paint store Monday, I'll show you a shade that matches her hair. She's got culture too—she sings in a choir at BYU."

Eric stood up.

"Where are you going?"

"I can't face another fried-bologna sandwich. I'm making me a peanut butter and jelly sandwich."

"Ever tried that broiled?" Hart asked, reaching over to confiscate Eric's unused fried bologna sandwich.

The day Eric left the mission field, Hart gave him a package to give his girl at BYU. It was a copy of his journal for her to type up so he could distribute copies at his homecoming. It was volume two of a six-volume set.

Three weeks after enrolling at the Y, Eric finally decided to get rid of the package.

When she opened the door, his mouth made funny sounds while he concentrated on her face. He wanted to take clay and model a copy of it so that he would always have it.

He explained about the package and gave it to her.

"Won't you come in?" she asked.

He knew he could fall in love with her, but he thought about his loyalty to a former companion. "No thanks."

Several times during the semester he saw her in the library. He would always stop and talk to her about Hart. It gave him a chance to study her face.

One day in January she phoned him.

"Leon will be home tomorrow," she said. "Can I ask a favor? Could you drive me to the Salt Lake airport to meet him? His parents will be driving down from Ogden, but I hate to ask them to drive to Provo first to get me. And I know he'd be happy to see you too."

Friday afternoon he picked her up at one o'clock. The clouds were heavy with moisture. By the time they arrived at the airport, the visibility was near zero.

The snow hit with a white fury.

They found Leon's parents and their three children in the terminal. They all crowded around Janice and chattered at once. Eric stood on the edge and smiled as though he were happy.

At first the announcements were that because of the weather the plane would be delayed. However, when it finally came, it flew over Utah without landing, continuing on its way to Los Angeles.

When the plane landed in Los Angeles, Leon called and left a message with the airlines desk that he would catch the next flight to Utah at nine-thirty.

The snow continued.

A little before seven, the youngest child fell down and cut her lip badly. Leon's parents rushed to the hospital. Eric and Janice were asked to wait at the airport for Leon.

At eight o'clock all flights were cancelled. By then it was impossible to leave the airport. Along with several hundred others, they were stranded in the airport for the night.

They found two empty chairs and sat down.

"You haven't talked much about your time with Leon," she said. "How long were you with him?"

"Six months, four days, and eight hours."

"So you must have really gotten close to him."

"Oh yes. He's a wonderful person—so neat and clean. We painted the kitchen four times while I was with him—couldn't get the right shade at first." He gave a forced laugh. "Of course I can laugh about it now."

"Did he tell you much about me?"

"All the time. He said you like yogurt too. I ate a lot of it while I was with him—I was getting an ulcer."

Her forehead furrowed. "Did you get along as companions?"

"Oh sure, we got along great."

She looked down. "Why are you making a fist?"

He relaxed his fingers. "Okay, maybe average. Well, there were a few problems at first, but with the help of our mission president, we worked them out."

"Problems? What kind of problems?"

"Nothing—there were no problems."

"Please tell me."

He tried to imagine her eating fried bologna sandwiches across the table from Leon. It was very depressing.

"Well, for one thing, he snores."

"Very bad?"

"Unbelievable—it shook the windows. But don't worry. I adjusted to it. You will too."

"How did you adjust?"

"I slept on the porch."

"In the winter too?"

"Actually they say it's healthy."

She stared down the long concourse hallway. "Of all the companions you had on your mission, how would you rate Leon?"

"He was the most tidy."

"But as far as your being able to get along with him, how would you rate him?"

He thought several seconds, then said, "That's not a fair question."

"Why isn't it?"

"It just isn't, that's all."

"Let me ask it another way. Would you have wanted to spend more time with him?"

He wiped his brow. "Golly, I learned so much from Leon—I don't think I could stand to learn another thing."

She started to chew on the thumb of her mitten.

"Please tell me the problems you had with him."

He lost his self-control. "Have you ever had fried bologna sandwiches and warm Jello for lunch every day for six months? Or painted a stupid kitchen four times? Other elders played basketball on their diversion day—we went to Sherwin Williams and compared color swatches!"

People were staring at him. Her face was ashen. She was nervously chewing on her mitten.

"I'm sorry," he apologized. "I don't know what got into me. I love Leon as a brother, and I wish you every happiness in your married life. Now please excuse me. I have to take a walk to cool down."

She went with him.

"Would you say he was considerate of your feelings?" she asked.

"I don't want to talk about him. I already feel rotten about what I've said. We had good times too, you know.

Teaching the gospel is too important to let little personality conflicts interfere. Okay, there were a few things that used to bug me, but I learned to forget things like that."

"What did you forget?"

"I forgot the gross way he used dental floss when we studied in the morning. Oh sure, I could understand him using it, but did he have to inspect everything he dragged out of his teeth? I forgot that."

"Oh no," she moaned.

"And I forgot the way he sucks food particles from his front teeth after every meal, and the same dumb expressions he uses over and over again. Dumb things like, 'Soup's on!' and 'Every cloud has a silver lining,' and 'Long time, no see.' I forgot all of that."

She pulled out a Kleenex and wiped her eyes.

"How did you meet him?" he asked.

"It was my freshman year. I'm from a small town, and I was scared to death. We were in the same ward. He talked me into majoring in English so I could teach school after we got married and he finished college. But after he left, I switched to music."

He stared at her hair. It was the color of ripe peaches. He wondered what it would be like to run his fingers through it.

"I know what you're thinking," she said.

"You do?" he asked warily.

"You're thinking—why major in music? What's so hard about singing songs? But it's more difficult than that."

"I'm sure it is."

"There's music theory, you know."

"Does Leon know about your major?"

"Not exactly. Tell me what else you forgot about him."

"There were so many things I forgot—I can't remember them all."

"Just one more?"

"You'll think it's such a little thing."

"I'd like to hear about it."

"Okay—one time I made a special dessert, a plum pudding. It took half our diversion day."

"I'd like to get your recipe," she said.

"But he just sat and wolfed it down, didn't say a word, mind you, then left the table sucking his teeth."

"Men are so thoughtless."

They looked at each other.

"I mean some people are so thoughtless," she said. "I don't think you're thoughtless. In fact, you seem like a warm and sensitive person."

He smashed his fist against the wall. He wasn't sure why.

"It's not important," he said quickly. "I've forgotten completely about it. It didn't bother me, not really. And I'm sure he'll compliment you on your cooking. You're probably a very good cook."

"I don't know how to make plum pudding."

"Take my advice—don't bother to learn."

It was now late at night. The airport chairs had been designed so one could not be comfortable in them very long. Eric placed his parka on the floor. They sat on it and leaned against the wall.

"Did you have someone who waited for you on your mission?" she asked.

"Yes. She's married now."

"Oh, I see."

"It was a returned missionary, you know," he said. "You have to watch out for them. All they're interested in is getting married. They don't care what poor hardworking elder they trample on when they take his girl."

"I know, I know."

He put his arm around her so she'd be more comfortable.

"Eric, what are you majoring in?"

"Physics. I want to help our country land a man on the moon, and in doing so, make the world a better place."

She grinned. "And the moon a poorer place."

"Once I thought about being a sculptor. When I look at your face, it makes me wish I were. You're very beautiful—technically speaking, of course."

"What made you change your mind about sculpturing?"

"It's not practical. Oh sure, I could get along by myself on what it'd bring in. But you can't raise a family being a sculptor. Besides, I'm an American, and in times like these, when our country needs scientists and engineers for the space race, I want to do what I can."

"That's very patriotic," she said.

"And it pays well," he said with a smile. "What are your goals in life?"

"Oh, you know, the usual. To get married in the temple, raise a family, and stay active in the Church."

"Sure," he said.

"And become the world's greatest female singer," she added with a smile.

"Don't laugh. It could happen."

"Well, I've had an offer to sing with the New Christy Minstrels."

"Are you going to do it?"

"I thought I'd see how things go with Leon and me."

The hours slipped by and they talked, going from earliest childhood memories to what they had for supper the night before.

At eleven o'clock she was paged for a phone message. Leon's parents had left the hospital and returned to Ogden for the night.

A few hours later, after her recital of songs from various musicals, after his explanation of why snow was white, they both fell asleep. He awoke at five-thirty with his arm around her, his nose very close to her hair. He sniffed. She smelled nice. With a contented smile, he fell asleep again.

She woke him at seven. "My back is killing me," she moaned. "Can we take a walk?"

He bought an orange and they shared it. She opened her mouth, and he placed a peeled section in it. She bit down; it squirted in his face. They both started giggling.

He was very happy.

Outside they could see large trucks carrying snow away from the runway. And the clouds were beginning to break.

"Are you engaged to Leon?"

"We've always talked about getting married after he got back."

"But you haven't signed anything, have you?"

"No."

"I see. Well, I just think there's something very special about the way we get along. Don't you?"

She nodded but didn't say anything.

At the ticket counter they found that the next plane from Los Angeles would arrive in an hour.

"I should go comb my hair and wash my face," she said.

"You're going to leave me, aren't you?"

"I told you—I have to go to the restroom and comb my hair and wash my face."

"Before you go, can I touch your face? Someday I want to do a sculpture of you."

"Will it take very long? Leon's on his way now."

He reached out with both hands and lightly traced the outlines of her face. "It's the cheekbones."

"I see," she said, trembling at his touch.

"Janice, I'm falling in love with you. Life's funny, isn't it?"

She backed away. "It isn't that funny."

"Okay, then," he complained, "if you want to be aloof, I can be aloof."

"That's it—I think we should be aloof."

"Terrific," he snapped. "I can be as aloof as the next person."

She ran her fingers over her face as if to erase the memory of his fingertips. "Somewhere up there is a plane with Leon on it. And in a few minutes, it'll land and Leon will come and take me away—and I'll listen to him snore for time and eternity."

She ran crying into the women's restroom.

When she returned, she phoned Leon's parents. Their driveway had drifted over during the night, and they couldn't get out. They asked if Eric could drive Leon home from the airport.

They walked to the gate where Leon's plane would land. She purposely sat two chairs from him while they waited. In a few minutes she fell asleep with her head dangling in space and her mouth open.

She began to snore.

He knew it was a bad position for sleep but decided for aloofness' sake against loaning her his shoulder.

A little later, Leon's plane was announced. Eric woke Janice up.

"My neck, my neck," she groaned. She hurried to the restroom to see if hot water would loosen it up.

A line of deplaning passengers began filing into the terminal.

Eric shook hands with Leon.

"Where are my parents, and where's Jan?"

Eric explained. "Elder, remember you're still on your mission till you report to your stake president. Arm's length, remember. And a simple handshake will do. Sometimes there are General Authorities of the Church in the airport, so watch yourself."

Janice came running out of the restroom, her head cocked at a funny angle, her neck still wet.

"Leon, Leon!" She held her arms out as she ran toward him.

"Don't touch me!" he shouted, looking with apprehension at an elderly man wearing a blue suit and carrying a briefcase.

She stopped, deeply disappointed.

Leon shook her hand. "Long time, no see, hey?"

They went to the airport restaurant for lunch. Leon

asked the waitress if they had fried bologna sandwiches. They didn't. He settled for soup.

Eric sat next to Janice on one side of the table with Leon on the other side.

"This is just like old times, hey?" Leon said heartily. "Us two eating together again."

Both Eric and Janice said yes at the same time.

"Jan, I really worked old Eric hard while he was with me. You can be sure of that."

"I always worked hard."

"Yeah," Leon chortled, "but you let down once in a while. Like when I suggested we paint the living room."

The waitress brought their food. Eric ordered some yogurt for himself.

"Well, soup's on!" Leon announced. He took several crackers from the tray and crushed them between his fingers into the soup.

"Jan, I got to hand it to you—waiting two years, typing up my journal for me, sending cookies once a month."

Eric quit eating. "Cookies? I don't remember any cookies."

"Leon had me send 'em in a shirt box, so that way . . ." Her voice trailed off.

Eric stared in shock at his former companion. "You held out on cookies? I can't believe it. How could you do that to me?"

"I didn't want you to get cavities."

"When did you eat 'em?"

"In the shower," Leon said.

Eric turned to Janice and complained. "He ate cookies without me."

"If you want," she said, "I'll make a batch just for you."

"I hardly think that would be appropriate," Leon said.

"Why not?" she asked.

"It's not right for a girl who's engaged to be baking cookies for another guy."

"I think we need to talk more about that," she said.

He paused. "Oh, all right—one batch of cookies, but that's all."

"Leon, that's not what we need to talk about."

"How could you not share the cookies she sent?" Eric complained. "I just want to say one thing, elder—I slaved all day once making you a nice plum pudding, and you didn't even have the decency to share your cookies with me."

"Plum pudding? What plum pudding?"

"Oh yeah?" Eric exploded. "And I suppose you don't remember the nice lemon sauce on top of it either."

"I don't remember any plum pudding."

Janice touched Leon's hand. He pulled away. "I'm sure it was a wonderful pudding. What harm is there in thanking Eric?"

"It couldn't have been too great if I can't even remember it."

Janice slumped in her chair. "Good grief, I feel like a marriage counselor."

When the waitress came by again, Janice ordered yogurt too.

Leon finished first, then sucked air between his front teeth to get out food particles. Apparently one fragment was particularly interesting, because he took it out of his mouth and examined it.

Eric looked at Janice and shrugged his shoulders.

After lunch they started to drive to Ogden. Progress was slow because of the snow.

On the way, Leon fell asleep. He began to snore. It sounded like a frog in an echo chamber.

"I can't stand it," Janice moaned. "If he and I were married, we'd have to live in separate houses."

"Janice, I know this is a little irregular, but will you marry me?"

"You're not serious!"

"I know, I know. It's too soon to ask. I wouldn't have asked today, but I know Leon will, and I wanted to get my bid in early."

"We hardly know each other."

"That's not true. Does Leon know you threw up the first day of kindergarten and ran home crying?"

"No, he doesn't know that."

"But I do—that's what two days of nonstop talking will do."

"I don't see how your knowing about my first day of kindergarten is pertinent to my deciding who I should marry."

"I know you better than Leon does. And I love you the way you are now—not the way you were two years ago. I love your face, your hair, the way you wrinkle up your nose when you question something."

"Well, I certainly question this, I'll tell you." She turned to face Leon. "It would break his heart if I didn't marry him."

"But you've changed so much since he's been gone."

She tried to close Leon's mouth to stop the snoring, but it was of no use. She stared at him as if he were an animal in a zoo.

"You're right," she finally admitted. "It's over between him and me. Two years to the day and now it's over."

"Poor guy," Eric said. "Oh well, look on the bright side. Every cloud has a silver lining."

A few minutes later Leon awoke to see Eric driving with his arm around Janice's shoulder.

"What are you two doing?"

"Oh, hi there," Eric said.

"You're just trying to get back at me for the cookies, aren't you!"

"That's not it. Leon, I love Janice, and if things work out I'm going to marry her." They drove in silence the rest of the way until Leon blurted out, "I've had a chance to think back and remember. And you know what?"

"What, Leon?"

"THE PLUM PUDDING WAS AWFUL!"

Three months later Eric and Janice were married in the Idaho Falls Temple.

CHAPTER SEVEN

After lunch Ryan and Michelle suggested that the three LDS couples skip the scheduled reunion activities and go for a hike. Janice and Ann backed down but encouraged the others to go.

C.J. took it upon himself to be the leader of the expedition. Eric stayed in the middle, with Ryan and Michelle content to lag behind.

It felt good to Eric to be outside, away from the telephone, away from the problems of others, out in the beauty of the mountains.

They stopped every few minutes to allow Ryan and Michelle to catch up.

Even at the first stop, the scenery was magnificent.

"We're dying, you know," C.J. said as they looked out at the mountains and valley below.

"What?"

"All of us will die. I guess I've always known it, but now I feel it. My father died in January."

"I'm sorry to hear that."

He took out a roll of antacid mints and tossed two into his mouth. "That was bad enough, but last month I turned forty."

"I guess it happens to all of us, doesn't it?"

"Do I look that old?"

"No, you look young. I wouldn't have thought you were forty."

"I use skin moisturizers. That's the key when you get old."

Eric nodded; he was bored by their conversation. "It's really nice up here, isn't it."

"You're a bishop, aren't you?"

"Yes, for the past four years."

"I suppose you get a lot of people coming to you with their problems."

"Sure."

"And I suppose you keep everything they say in confidence, don't you?"

"Right. Look over there at the way the shadows play across that ridge."

"What sort of problems do people bring you?"

"All kinds. I can just make out a little stream in that valley. I should have brought my fishing pole. When's the last time you had brook trout?"

"Two years ago," C.J. said, "I committed adultery."

Suddenly the sky turned gray for Eric.

"Oh," he said. "Talk to your own bishop—he can help you."

"I can't talk to my bishop."

"Why not?"

"I'm afraid he'd excommunicate me from the Church. But I need to talk to someone. It's given me an ulcer carrying it all by myself. It happened two years ago at a meeting in New York. The woman was from Iowa, I think. I can't remember her name except it was the name of a flower—Rose or Daisy or Violet. I can't remember."

Eric tried to focus on the stream in the valley, but it was no use. All he could think about was Ann.

"It didn't mean anything to me. I didn't enjoy it. And I felt guilty afterwards. My ulcer just kills me sometimes. It was just the one time. I'll never do it again. It wasn't worth it. I've learned my lesson."

"You have to talk to your bishop about it."

"He's busy—I hate to bother him."

"There's no other way."

"What's so important about talking to him?"

"Because you've been through the temple and made a

solemn promise before God that you'd never be unfaithful to your wife. Now you've broken that promise. A bishop is a judge, and he needs to find the way for you to repent so the transgression can be forgiven, so you can take advantage of the Savior's atonement."

Down the trail they could hear Ryan and Michelle singing a hiking song.

"I've prayed about it. That should be enough. I don't see why I have to let the bishop in on it."

"Because you've not only offended God, you've offended the Church. Forgiveness ultimately comes from God, but the bishop must be approached, especially for somebody who's been through the temple."

"If I went to him, and if he excommunicated me and everyone found out, it'd break Ann's heart. She might divorce me, and then I'd lose her and the kids. All that for a mistake I made just one time. Besides that, I manage the store, like I told you, but it really belongs to Ann's father. There's no way he'd let me continue working there if Ann divorced me. I'm forty years old. I can't start all over again selling waterless cookware."

Ryan and Michelle finally caught up with them.

"Sorry," Michelle gasped, sitting down to rest. "The reason we took so long was that Ryan and I were down there kissing like crazy. Isn't that right, kiddo?"

Ryan sat beside her and grinned. "I deny everything."

Michelle pulled out a picture and gave it to Eric. "This is our son. He's on a mission in Argentina. What do you think?"

Eric looked at the handsome young man in white shirt and tie standing outside the mission home. He had his father's self-confidence.

"You must be very proud of him," Eric said, handing back the picture.

"He still holds the state record for the mile," Ryan said. "And he's always been strong in the Church. You know, I was thinking today. Where would we be if we weren't members of the Church?"

C.J. stood up. "We'd better get going." He started up the hill again.

"What a taskmaster," Michelle joked.

They continued up the trail. Before long Michelle and Ryan were behind Eric. He found C.J. waiting for him a little ways up the trail.

"It's not right to excommunicate somebody for one little mistake—for just one time."

"It's not a little mistake, even if it was only once. The only sin more serious than adultery is murder."

"I don't believe that. It can't be that bad."

"Why not?"

"Because a lot of basically good people do it. It can't be number two. What's the harm if nobody gets hurt?"

"Somebody got hurt, C.J."

"Who? Ann doesn't know about it. The other woman isn't at all religious. So who got hurt?"

"You did, and you're still hurting, and you always will till you go through the steps of repentance. First you have to go to your bishop."

"What will he do?"

"I don't know. I'm not your bishop."

"What would you do?"

"I'd phone the stake president to see if he wanted to go ahead with a high council court."

C.J. groaned. "The high council? I can't go to the high council. Now we've gone from one person knowing about it to twelve."

"They keep these things in confidence."

"It doesn't matter if they do or not, because Ann's father is on the high council."

"Oh," Eric said.

"Now you see why I can't go to my bishop. This is a special case. If I went, it would end up destroying Ann and my marriage and our children's confidence in me and my career. I can't do it. It's too big a price to pay."

"Too bad you didn't count the price two years ago in that hotel room, isn't it."

C.J. shot away from him up the hill.

It's not my problem, Eric told himself.

At the same time he worried about Ann.

For the rest of the hike Eric stayed with Ryan and Michelle. She told him about coaching a girls' softball team.

* * * * *

When he returned to their room, Janice was taking a nap. He decided to make some phone calls downstairs.

First he called his first counselor, who said right off, "Bishop, we've got a problem."

"What?"

"The state bee inspector found foul brood disease in our bees. He burned ten hives so they wouldn't infect the others. President Baxter found out, and he's really upset. He said if we'd used the Terramycin in April when the stake suggested it, our hives would be okay now."

Eric felt his stomach churning.

Next he phoned his next-door neighbor.

"Mort, could you do me a favor and go to our place and make sure nobody's broken in? The key is under the welcome mat. I'll wait."

A few minutes later, Mort returned.

"I couldn't find the key, Eric."

"It's under the welcome mat."

"That's just it. I couldn't find the welcome mat."

"Mort," he said, starting to lose control, "it says *Welcome.*"

"I guess the group who painted your house must have moved it."

"What group?"

"After you left, about twenty high school kids came over and painted your house. I thought you knew about it."

"What color did they paint it?"

"Sort of a garden-hose green, you know, real bright and plastic looking."

"How does it look, Mort?"

"Like a garden hose."

Eric moaned. For months he had been after the Laurels and priests to get a service project.

"Mort, does it go with the ornamental brick facing we have on the front of the house?"

"Yep, goes with it perfectly."

Eric gave a sigh of relief. Maybe it wouldn't be that bad to live with.

"Because they painted over that too," Mort added.

Eric said goodbye and hung up. If there was ever a reason to drink, he thought as he walked to the snack bar, this weekend is it.

He ordered a milkshake. A group of classmates sat talking at a table. He decided to sit down and listen for a while.

They were playing a game called "Can You Top This." "At first," one confessed humbly, "I didn't feel ready to take over as chairman of the board, but they said I was the best man for the job. That was four years ago. Last week we closed one deal for 80 million dollars."

A while later, someone else took the challenge. "It's funny how I even got started producing movies. I was just sitting there one day with a friend telling about what a rotten movie I'd seen the night before. He bet me I couldn't do any better. Well, I decided to take him up. Sure, at first I didn't know anything—no college education, just three years of surfing on the beach. The first movie we did was about surfing, you know. Well, one thing led to another, and our last movie grossed thirty million. But the thing is, I still think about the good times we had in high school . . . "

Eric nursed his milkshake, his head down to avoid anyone noticing him.

Just then Bucky Barnes sat down, saw Eric, and started laughing. Then he started singing, "I'm looking over a four-leaf clover . . . " Eric walked out.

He ended up at the corral watching the horses being saddled by a teenage ranch hand.

He stared at the mountain.

Suddenly he was at the Guggenheim Museum with Barbara Walters on TV. This was the unveiling ceremony of his ice sculpture. Many of his high school classmates were there.

" . . . always knew he had great potential," Bucky told Barbara. It was time for the unveiling.

Eric turned to a museum staff member. "Was it hard to figure out a way to keep the sculpture below freezing?"

"What are you talking about?" the man said.

"And now for the moment the world has been waiting for," Barbara said.

"No, wait! Something's gone wrong!"

Barbara dropped the sheet away. There was just a puddle of water under the sheet.

" . . . always knew he'd be a failure," Bucky told Barbara.

He decided to see if Janice was awake from her nap. As he walked through the lobby on the way to his room, someone called out his name. He turned to face Gary Martin, his best friend in high school, his competition in math and science classes.

Gary, who twenty years ago had thick glasses and wore a slide rule like a holster from his belt, who read *Scientific American* from cover to cover and talked about it to others—now had a full, well-trimmed beard, and a pipe that he could use to stop conversations as people stopped to watch him clean it, fill it with a rich-smelling tobacco, then light it. It was his way of slowing down the world while he thought.

"Nothing like being on time," Eric joked, noticing the suitcase in Gary's hand.

"We had car trouble last night and had to stay overnight in some one-horse town."

Eric met Gary's wife, Eileen, a tired-looking woman.

As they talked, Eric learned that Gary had also finished his Ph.D. in physics, but had fared better than Eric. He was now the department chairman in a small college.

"What are you doing?" he asked.

Eric rehearsed his story.

"Lawn Doctor? That's really an indictment of our society, you know. A man with your training and potential—I just can't believe it. Here you are, wasting your life when you could be contributing to society." He took a large puff from his pipe and slowly exhaled. "I'm looking for someone to fill a vacancy for the fall. Why don't you come and work with us at Midwestern?"

"I'm tired of one-year appointments," Eric said.

"This'd be a permanent position. Assistant professor—a tenure track position."

"Why would you offer me a job? I haven't done any physics for years."

"You'll pick it up again. Whadaya say? Us together working—challenging each other to new heights."

"I can't believe this is happening."

"Well, are you interested?"

"Sure, I'm interested. In fact, I'll take the job. I guess I should talk to my wife first, though."

He returned to their room. Janice was still sleeping. He sat on the bed and looked at the mountain peak.

He stood in a large amphitheater filled with students. They had come with notebooks in hand to learn the secrets of the universe. They were all eagerly waiting for him to appear. This morning there would also be representatives from the news media because of his being named winner of a Nobel Prize in science.

Barbara Walters, on camera, stepped forward. "Eric, may I join with the American people to congratulate you on your Nobel Prize. This must be a very happy day for you. How will you be spending it?"

He looked sincerely into the camera. "I'll spend it the way I spend every day—trying to advance man's knowledge of the universe, and training the future scientists of the world with insight and wisdom."

"What an example for all of us," she said, touching him on the sleeve.

"I'm very happy because now my life has meaning. There's a pattern to it. At first the fabric looked random like some rich Oriental rug. But as the years have passed, I've seen a pattern emerging. That's what's important—that there be a pattern, that there be meaning and purpose to our professional life. And I've found it, you see. Of course, the Nobel Prize is nice, but the best part is to know that my education was not wasted. Yes, Barb, it's a good life."

*　　*　　*　　*　　*

Janice awoke at five o'clock. "Did you have a nice hike?" she asked.

"Janice, I need to talk to you."

"Just a minute. I have to go to the bathroom. The baby's sitting on my bladder again."

In a minute she was back.

"I have some good news and some bad news." He smiled, trying to restrain his happiness. "What do you want first?"

"The bad news," she yawned.

"They painted our house."

"Who did?"

"The kids from church. They needed a service project."

"What color?"

"Garden-hose green."

"Does it go with the bricks?"

"They painted the bricks too."

"You'll have 'em repaint it like it was before, won't you?"

"It'd hurt their feelings."

"I don't care about their feelings. I'm not living in a garden hose."

"Now for the good news. It doesn't matter about the house, because we're going to sell it and move. I met an old friend of mine this afternoon. He's department head at Midwestern College in Minnesota. He offered me a permanent position there teaching. Isn't that fantastic?"

Janice sat up in bed. "Oh," she said.

"You like the idea, don't you?" he asked.

"Oh . . . moving again," she mumbled.

"Don't you see? This'll give meaning to my life. You know, to get all that schooling and not use it was a waste. But now, it'll all fall into place—my life will make sense now, like the pattern from an Oriental rug."

Janice was biting her lower lip and searching for a Kleenex. "An Oriental rug?" she repeated.

"And you'll be a faculty wife. They'll have a club for you to go to, and you can take classes for free if you want, and people in the community will respect us, and we'll have a nice home with a study for me. You'll see, it'll be fine for us. I wonder what classes I'll be teaching in the fall."

"This fall?"

"Actually, classes start the last week of August."

"Oh," she said quietly, wiping her eyes.

"I'm really excited about this. I know it'll take a lot of work to sell our house and pack and sell the business, but we can do it."

Janice looked out the window at the mountain.

"Janice, I have to do this, don't you see?"

Janice wiped her eyes.

"I'd better go find out what classes I'll be teaching."

He got Gary's room number from the desk clerk.

Gary's wife answered his knock.

"Gary's not here. He went to do some work on the car. If you want, I'll show you where he is. He parked it in the shade."

They went outside.

"Gary says you'll be coming to teach in the fall."

"Yes, I can hardly wait."

"Sure," she said without much enthusiasm.

"Gary's working on his own car?" Eric asked.

"Something about the timing. It runs real bad."

"It's sort of a hobby with him?" Eric asked.

"Hobby? We're just trying to save a little money. You know, after I started working, we had to get a second car; then there was the cost of a baby sitter. We're hardly any better off now than we were before."

"Oh," Eric said.

"You see, every year the state legislature approves a six percent raise. With a twelve percent inflation rate, it doesn't take long to figure out what that does to a standard of living."

"I see."

"Where were you teaching last year?" she asked.

"I wasn't. I've been in business for myself."

"Business, that's the ticket—where your income is limited only to what you produce, and where you're your own boss and don't have to worry about what the board of regents or the governor dreams up. Yes sir, having your own business is the way to go."

"But your husband is a professional. He has stature, and people respect him for his education."

She laughed. "Gary? Mostly he teaches service courses. Kids have to take two semesters to fulfill a requirement, but that's all. Gary calls it Physics for Non-Believers. They resent having to learn the material, and as soon as they've had the course, he never sees 'em again. Tell me, what do you expect from this job anyway?"

Eric didn't have time to answer. They came upon Gary bent over the car.

"Have you got it fixed yet?" his wife asked.

"No, not yet."

"You know, it's no crime to ask a real mechanic to fix it, somebody who knows what he's doing."

"Well, thanks a lot!" Gary exploded. "I try and save a little money, and what appreciation do you give me?"

She shrugged her shoulders and left.

"I told Janice about the job," Eric said. "She's a little stunned, but I think she's going to like it. I'll put my business on the market as soon as we get home. Now you're sure you'll be able to hire me permanently?"

"No problem. I've figured out how to get around the red tape."

Eric paused, then asked, "What red tape?"

Gary fought a stuck bolt. "Oh nothing. It's just that there's a man in our department named Perkins. He figures he should have been chosen as department head. He fights me tooth and nail on everything. See, the problem is that the position we've advertised is for a one-year contract."

"I don't want a one-year contract."

"I know. It'll be permanent. Here's how we'll do it. Perkins is scheduled for a sabbatical next year. So when he goes, I'll push for your position being permanent. Now Perkins' cronies Smith and Ranley will fight it, but they won't have the votes. And when Perkins gets back, Ranley will go on sabbatical, so we'll still have the votes. Don't worry."

"Gary, it sounds shaky. Is there anything else I should know?"

"Nothing important—oh, the governor is in a power struggle with the board of regents, but I don't think anything'll come of it."

"What could come of it—the worst possible case?"

"Well, there's been talk about turning us into a service department and having all our majors go to State."

"What if that happens?"

"It won't happen, but if it did, I guess we'd be overstaffed."

"It sounds like a hornets' nest. Does anybody ever have any time to teach?"

"It's not that bad. It's just something that happens every year."

The nut wouldn't turn no matter how hard he tried. He swore.

"Gary, how much will my position in your department pay?"

Gary named a figure.

"That's all?"

"Well, it's only a nine-month contract, so you can do whatever you want to earn money in the summer."

"How about if we make it an eleven-month contract with more money."

"No, that's not possible."

"That'd be a real cut in pay for me, Gary."

"Well, that's as an assistant professor. In time, you'll be promoted to associate professor."

"How much time?"

"A minimum of five years. That's after you get tenure."

"And how much does associate professor pay?"

Gary named a figure.

Eric paused, then asked, "How much does a full professor get?"

Gary named another figure.

"I make more off Orange Julius than a full professor's salary."

"It shows what a poor sense of values we have in this country."

Eric paused, then said, "I'm not sure that's what it shows, Gary."

"That a person can earn more selling orange juice than he can teaching in the sciences? What do you think it shows?"

"I think it shows how effective I am in what I do. That's what I think it shows. Gary, why are you so anxious to have me come and work for you?"

Gary quit fighting the car and looked up. "In high school, we were a team. You remember the plans and dreams we had of really making a contribution to science, something that'd improve the world some way. You remember the long discussions we had at night doing our math homework, how we'd argue whether light was a particle or a wave—the excitement we had about science then, the thrill of learning the basic principles of the universe. Do you remember that, Eric?"

Eric nodded his head soberly. "I remember."

"Well, I've lost it. I've lost the excitement and the curiosity and the drive. Instead of doing significant research, I do safe work, good enough to get published in some mediocre journal. As department head, my life is filled with endless meetings and zero base budgeting, and checklists and goal sheets, and class schedules. And none of it is part of the dream I had about my life so long ago."

"I know," Eric said quietly.

"That's why I want you to come to Midwestern—to see if we can be a team again and make reality the dreams we had when we were young." Gary wiped his forehead. "Before I die, I want to do something worthwhile. Somewhere I've lost the dreams of youth."

"Gary," Eric confessed, "I've lost 'em too."

Gary nodded. "Sure—it was too much to ask. It sounds like maybe you're not that interested in the position anymore."

"I guess I'm not. Maybe I'm better off as Lawn Doctor. But thanks for thinking of me."

"What a waste of talent," Gary said. He strained at the wrench; it broke loose, and he smashed his fist into the motor block.

* * * * *

Eric returned to Janice. She had been crying.

"I'm not taking the teaching job," he said.

"Why not?"

"I'm not the person he wanted. He wanted me the way I was twenty years ago."

"Are you sad about not taking the job?"

"You know what I've decided? My life isn't the way I planned it, but it's really a pretty good life, isn't it? I'm my own boss. I work hard. I put food on the table and I work in the Church. I'm not perfect, but they can't fault me for not trying. I try hard."

He lay down beside her.

"Janice," he said, whispering in her ear, "I think my life hasn't turned out so bad. I'm not going to be ashamed anymore."

There was a knock on the door.

With the covers pulled over their heads, they could hardly hear the knocking at all.

"Eric," she whispered, "sometime, not now, I need to tell you about *H.M.S. Pinafore.*"

"Later, Janice, later."

CHAPTER EIGHT

The Saturday banquet and dance were to be the culmination of the reunion.

Eric and Janice entered the dining room during Happy Hour. Ryan and Michelle were circulating through the crowd with milkshakes in their hands, inviting people to the church service the next morning. C.J. and Ann sat alone at a table, waiting for supper. C.J. stared at a half-empty package of antacid tablets.

Eric and Janice found a snack table with sausage rolls. They filled a plate and began to walk around the crowded room.

"Eric, how's it going?"

Eric turned to face a man wearing a designer jump suit. It was Ron Harper. During high school, they had worked together in a furniture warehouse one summer.

"Ron, good to see you. This is my wife, Janice."

"Looks just like Martha Wilson, doesn't she?"

Janice smiled. "Several people think so. Could you send Martha over to us if you see her?"

"Sure will, if I see her."

"Is your wife here?"

"No—I'm between wives right now. The divorce went through three months ago. It was the best thing in the world. Now I'm free to do what I want."

"What do you want?" Eric asked.

"I want to get married again," he said. "I'm looking around tonight, but they're all too old for me here at the reunion."

"But they're your same age," Janice said.

"I know—that's too old. Each time I get married I like to drop down another few years below my age. Funny how it works out. The first one was my age, twenty. The second one, when I was twenty-nine, was twenty-two. The third one was only nineteen. Her dad and I used to play a lot of golf together. It didn't last though—I mean the marriage—I still play golf with her dad. And would you believe now that I'm pushing forty, I'm dating a twenty-three-year-old stewardess. I figure it's a way of never aging."

Janice stared at him as if he were from another world.

"What was wrong with the first three?" she asked.

"Oh, you know, the usual things. We quit talking to each other. And, I don't know, marriage seemed to age 'em. They weren't as much fun after a year or two. Hey, who's that blonde over there?"

It was The Blonde. Eric sighed. "I don't know. Tell me if you find out."

"Excuse me," Ron said, leaving to track down the blonde.

"Men," Janice scowled.

"Some men," Eric corrected.

They went to get another plate of sausage rolls.

"Eric! Man, is it good to see you!"

He turned to face Del Ackerman, an old neighborhood friend.

They said the usual preliminary things.

Del introduced them to his wife, Elaine.

"What are you doing, Eric?"

"I'm in business for myself."

"Terrific. What kind of business?"

Eric told him.

"No kidding! And you're making it okay?"

"We're doing all right."

"I'm impressed."

"You are?"

"Sure. Anyone who can make it in this economy has got to be good."

"You know, that's true, isn't it? Thanks, Del. I needed that."

"It reminds me of something that happened to me about ten years ago. We'd just moved to California, you see . . . "

"It was twelve years ago," his wife said.

"Twelve years? No, it was in '71."

"It was '69, Del," Elaine said sharply.

"How do you know?"

"Because I'd just had a baby, that's why. I remember nursing Todd in that empty house. The furniture didn't come for a week."

"Yeah, they sent it to Detroit by mistake."

"Cleveland," his wife corrected.

"Let me tell the story, okay?" Del barked. "After, if you want, you can pass out a correction sheet."

"Go ahead—tell the story. It's not that great anyway."

Del shook his head. "Forget the story then."

Elaine erupted. "If you say you're going to tell a story, then tell it!"

"You always have to be on my case, don't you? You're always at me for something. Now it's that crazy psycho retreat. Eric, let me ask you something. Does your wife bug you to leave for two months to go to a self-awareness seminar where they sit in mud baths and discuss where they're coming from?"

"Del, I need space," his wife said.

"Then get a job as a forest ranger, for crying out loud! But don't sit in a mud puddle for two weeks and look at your skin pucker up. Of all the stupid . . . "

Eric and Janice excused themselves. They got some more sausage rolls and stood on the edge of the group and watched.

A woman came over to Eric. She looked like a twin to Janice.

"You must be Martha Wilson," Eric said.

"Yes, I am. My married name is Elliot."

"You two do look alike," Eric said, comparing them.

"My husband would like to see you. Could you follow me?"

They followed her. On the other side of the room off to the side was a man in a wheelchair. It was Brad Elliott, a former high school track runner.

Eric shook Brad's left hand because he had no right hand, and no legs either.

"You've got a good-looking wife, Eric," he said with a grin.

"I think we both have good taste."

"Thanks. She's been everything to me. You never went to Viet Nam, did you, Eric?"

"No, I didn't."

"I was there three months. Part of me is still there," he said.

"I'm sorry, Brad. I didn't know."

"Nobody knew. How did you get out of it? You must have been eligible."

"When they were doing a lot of drafting, I was in college so I was deferred. Then after that, I went to graduate school."

"Well, there were lots of things a person could do to get out of it."

"I'm sorry, Brad."

"Sorry? For what?"

"Sorry about your legs and your hand—sorry I let you go in my place."

"So you could get blown up?"

"I don't know what I mean."

"Nobody knows. I've never talked to anyone who knew anything about Viet Nam. So don't talk about it. Especially don't say you know what it was like—okay?"

"Okay."

"If it weren't for Martha, I'd have put myself away.

We have a six-year-old daughter. She's a honey. Do you have any kids?"

"Four and a half," Eric answered.

"Good. Kids are nice."

"Brad, will you come to our church service tomorrow?"

"What for?"

"It's the only thing I could give you that'd ever amount to a hill of beans. It's about your family, Brad."

"Maybe I will."

By the time the salads were served, the three LDS couples were seated together. "This missionary work is fun," Michelle bubbled. "We've asked scads of people to our church service tomorrow."

"Don't get your hopes up too high," Eric warned.

She countered with a smile. "And don't get yours down too low, bishop."

"Everybody look at C.J.," Ann said happily. "We have a little secret, don't we, dear?"

C.J.'s hand shot out for another antacid tablet.

"What secret?" Michelle asked.

"You tell 'em, C.J.," she said.

"Tell 'em what?" he croaked, wiping his forehead.

"About your suit, silly."

C.J. took a long drink of water.

Ann touched the fabric. "It was just unbelievably wrinkled when I got it out this afternoon while you were all on your hike. I guess it had fallen off the hanger in the garment bag. It was such a mess. Well, guess what I did? I hung the slacks from the curtain rod in our bathroom and ran a hot shower for ten minutes with the door closed. You would not believe the difference it made. It's like sending it to the cleaners, but much cheaper."

"It looks very nice," Janice said.

"And C.J. does too, doesn't he?" Ann said proudly. "How old do you think he is?"

"Forty," Eric said.

Ann was disappointed. "Yes, he is—he's forty. But do you think he looks forty?"

They all looked at C.J. He was supporting his head with his hand, staring down at the table.

"No," Michelle said. "He doesn't look forty to me."

"Do you know why?" Ann asked. "It's because of the facial mask we use once a week. What we do is take a cube of fresh yeast and mix it with enough warm water to make it creamy. Then squeeze an orange peel into it, add a tablespoon of honey, and half a mashed avocado; then we put the mixture on our faces for twenty minutes, then rinse with warm water."

"Ann," C.J. interrupted, "I'm sure they don't want to know about that."

"Why not? They'll all be forty someday."

Ryan laughed. "It'll take more than turning forty before I'll put a mashed avocado on my face for twenty minutes."

"You can laugh if you want," Ann said, "but I can see the aging in Eric's face, and if he used an avocado-yeast mixture, it wouldn't be so noticeable."

"It's a good thing you're both LDS," Janice said, "because some women'd worry if their husbands looked too young."

Ann laughed.

C.J. and Eric did not.

After the meal, there was a program chaired by Jerry Lampen, former high school fullback, now an insurance executive in California.

Jerry warmed up things with a few crude jokes.

Next came the skits titled "Name that Classmate."

The first few were easy enough. The first one spotlighted their Hollywood producer; the next skit was about the person in their class who had marketed "Pet Potatoes" and made a fortune.

Then came the third skit.

Two men in white lab coats hurriedly wheeled in a service tray covered over with a white sheet. Another man in white coat brought a tray of tools covered by a cloth. A third man entered, obviously a doctor. He prepared to do an operation.

A woman ran sobbing hysterically toward the doctor.

"Oh, doctor, can you save my baby? Please, doctor!"

Eric began to blush. He felt heat rushing through his body, and sweat began erupting everywhere.

After some more theatrics, the doctor removed the white sheet from the cart to reveal several inches of sodded lawn.

"Okay, gang, who is that class member?"

"I know! I know!"

Bucky Barnes staggered to his feet. "That's our great scientist, Doctor Eric Turner. Do you know what he does now? He mows lawns and has a lemonade stand!"

"That's right!" Jerry announced. "Let's hear it for Lawn Doctor!"

The crowd clapped. Eric stood and waved, all smiles, then sat down.

They gave him a prize for being a good sport—a bag of fertilizer.

"Well, gang," Jerry continued, "now it's time to get a little more serious. You know, we had—I think you'll all agree with me on this—we had something real special in our class. I think we were all, well, a pretty great bunch of kids. Now let's see how we turned out as a class. How many lawyers do we have out there tonight? Hey? C'mon, you lawyers, stand up!"

Four men stood up.

"Hey, that's terrific! Let's hear it for our lawyers!" Applause. "Okay, now how many physicians are in our class?"

Two men and one woman stood up.

"Terrific! Isn't that fantastic? Now how many scientists and engineers do we have out there?"

Six men stood up.

Jerry proceeded through the rest of his list: bank officers, mayors, politicians, business executives.

Eric sat in his chair and stared at his water glass. Janice put her arm on his hand to comfort him.

A minute later Jerry quit, but he promised to be back.

"That wasn't fair," Michelle complained.

"I'm so mad," Janice fumed. "I wanted to grab that microphone and ask some questions of my own. How many men out there are good fathers? How many go to work, day in and day out, doing the best they know how, not because the work is glamorous or fun, but because their family depends on them? How many small businessmen do we have out there who start a business from scratch and through hard work finally make it profitable? How many fathers keep putting off buying a new car so their kids can have braces or take music lessons? And how many husbands have been faithful to their wives all the time they've been married?"

"We're so lucky to have the husbands we have," Ann said proudly.

C.J. excused himself and left the table. Eric followed him out.

He found C.J. at the candy machine looking for some antacid tablets.

"My stomach is killing me," he complained.

"I told you what you need to do to find relief."

"I can't do that," he said.

A few minutes later Eric returned to the table.

"How are you doing, bishop, after that terrible skit?" Michelle asked.

"To think I came three hundred miles for an insult and a bag of fertilizer," he said with a slight grin.

When the dance started, Eric held Janice in his arms, his eyes closed, trying to ignore the bulge in her stomach.

"Bishop, I love you," she whispered in his ear.

The dance ended and they started walking back to their table.

"Eric, can I have this dance?" The Blonde asked. "For old times' sake?"

Eric looked sheepishly at Janice.

"Oh sure, go ahead," Janice said. "I know you two have a lot to talk about."

The Blonde melted into his arms as the music started.

"Have you tried any of the sausage rolls at the snack table?" Eric asked nervously, embarrassed at having her so close to him. "I think we should go over right now and get some before they run out."

She started laughing. "You're trying to weasel out of dancing with me, aren't you? After all the time we spent together our senior year."

"Who are you?" Eric asked.

"Jane Samuels. Don't you remember? I was the secretary of science club."

Eric remembered the girl who took minutes at their meetings. She was a plain-looking girl, with short, dull brown hair and gray glasses and dumpy clothes. Before him stood the exact opposite.

"Is that you in there, Jane?" he asked.

She laughed again, delighted with her little joke against nature.

"Renew an old friendship?" Janice asked when he returned to the table a few minutes later.

"She was science club secretary, but she was very plain then."

"Sure she was," Janice said, unconvinced.

An hour later, the band took its first break. Jerry returned.

"Hey, gang, are we having fun!" Applause. "It reminds me of the . . . "

The joke ended, the crowd roared.

"I don't get it," Janice complained.

"It's just as well," Eric replied.

"Gang, we've got some awards to give out now. Our first award goes to the class member who traveled the farthest to come to our reunion. It goes to Marty Walder, who came here all the way from Kenya, Africa. C'mon up here, Marty, and get your prize! Hey, gang, let's hear it for Marty!"

Marty went up and received his pen and pencil set.

"Our next award goes to the couple who've been married the longest. Stand up if you've been married longer than seventeen years."

Ryan and Michelle stood up, along with several others.

"Okay, let's narrow it down a little. How about twenty years?"

Ryan and Michelle were the only ones standing.

"Hey, we got a winner! Ryan and Michelle—come on up and get your prize!"

As they walked to the front, Bucky staggered to his feet, and heckled them. "Yeah, and while you're up, tell us why you got married so young!"

There was a roar of laughter.

Ryan good-naturedly took the prize, gave it to Michelle, then grabbed the microphone and waited for them to quiet down.

"Okay, okay," he said. "You all know we had to get married. We knew we'd take some flack from some of you this weekend, but we came anyway because we wanted you to know we're still together. I love my wife. And a thousand years from now, I'll still love her." He kissed her.

"Hey, none of that!" Jerry kidded.

"Why not?" Ryan grinned. "It's a lot more wholesome than your jokes."

Laughter.

After they quieted down, Ryan handed the microphone to Michelle.

She took a big breath and began. "It's hard to believe you were the ones who made me feel so bad. I guess I'll never forget what I heard some of you say behind my back when I got pregnant."

It became very quiet.

"But time passes. I want you to know that our oldest child, the baby I was pregnant with in high school, is now a fine young man, tall and muscular like his dad. He played baseball and football in high school. Right now he's a missionary for The Church of Jesus Christ of Latter-day Saints, working at his own expense to tell people about our church."

She reached for Ryan's hand.

"After we got married, we joined the Mormon Church. A year later we went to one of their temples and knelt across an altar and extended out marriage even beyond this life. We will always be married.

"And that's why we came here this weekend—to tell you about our happiness. Tomorrow morning in this room, we're having a little church service. Anybody who wants to come is welcome. And if you can't come, we have some pamphlets on the fireplace mantel for you. Jerry, thanks for letting us talk. I think you're doing one tremendous job as an M.C. tonight. Well, isn't he?"

The crowd applauded.

Jerry kissed Michelle on the cheek and shook hands with Ryan as they turned to leave.

Through the rest of the dance, Eric danced as close as he could to Janice.

During a break in the dancing, C.J. asked to speak to Eric in the hall.

"It was only one time. Why make a fuss about one time? I learned my lesson. I'll never do it again, so there's no need for me to see my bishop."

"One time is too many. You need to go through the repentance process—and part of that is talking to your bishop."

"It's too much to ask."

"Things'll work out if you do it the Lord's way."

"Before I talked to my bishop, I'd have to tell Ann. I don't see how I can do that. Maybe I'll just wait for a good time to tell her."

"I don't think there is a good time to tell your wife you've committed adultery. You just have to do it. Within a couple of weeks, okay?"

"Maybe."

Finally the dance was over. Eric and Janice went to their room, hand in hand.

"Tonight are you going to wear the nightgown?" he asked.

"Whatever you say," she said with a smile. "You deserve something more than a bag of fertilizer. And I deserve something more than watching you dance with that blonde."

She went into the bathroom to brush her teeth. To get just the right atmosphere, he draped his shirt over the lampshade of the bedside lamp, then turned out the overhead light.

She opened the door. She was wearing the new nightgown.

They knelt down for prayers.

There was a knock at the door.

C.J. called out on the other side of the door. "Bishop? Are you awake? It's very important."

Janice put on her robe and stepped into the bathroom.

Eric got dressed and opened the door.

"Bishop, I've got to talk to you."

Eric let him in.

"I told Ann about what happened two years ago."

"I thought you'd wait till you got back home."

"There's no TV in the room—we had to talk about something."

"How did she take it?"

"It was like she didn't hear me. She's just been sitting there on the bed, rocking back and forth, with her hands folded in front of her. I don't know what to do now."

Janice came out of the bathroom. "Hi there, C.J. How are you tonight?"

"Just fine."

"Would you like some Girl Scout cookies?"

"No thanks."

She rummaged through a box. "I've still got a few mints. You know, the mints went the fastest."

She passed him the box. He took a mint.

"C.J. and I need to talk."

"Okay, I'll go back to the bathroom."

"No, you stay here and we'll talk in the bathroom."

"Fine—I'll just slip into bed and read my skiing magazine."

C.J. went and got two chairs from his room, which they set up in the bathroom.

For a while neither one said anything.

"The toilet leaks, doesn't it," C.J. said.

"Yes."

"That'll waste a lot of water in a year."

"Sure."

"Energy too, if it's hot water."

"Right."

C.J. opened the top and looked into the water closet with all its levers.

"My dad," he said, "could fix anything. One time we were on vacation and we stopped at a motel and the toilet didn't work right. He went out to the car for his tool chest and came in and fixed it. And he never said a word to the manager about it. He just fixed it. He was that way, you know. I miss him so much now that he's dead."

C.J. flushed the toilet several times, watching the mechanism work.

Finally he looked up. "Forty years old and I don't know how to fix a toilet."

"Me neither, C.J."

"My dad would, though."

"Sure."

C.J. sat down. "We were always so different from each other, you know. He must really be disappointed in me, in what I've become. He never wore anything to church but the same blue suit, and he'd drive a car till it rusted out. He wasn't a bit image conscious. Now look at his son—an image consultant. What must he think about me now that he's dead and can see behind my cardboard front—especially if he knows what I've done?"

"At least now he'll know you're trying to repent."

They decided to take a walk. They walked in the moonlight along a gravel road that might have led to the mountain if they'd kept on it long enough.

"I keep asking myself—why did I get involved with that woman two years ago?"

"Why did you?"

"She was younger than me. Maybe that was important to me—to feel like I could attract a younger woman. I don't know. I guess I'll spend the rest of my life wondering how I could have been so stupid."

"If you go through the process of repentance suggested by your bishop, there'll come a time in your life when you'll feel the Lord has forgiven you. When that happens, you must not dwell anymore on it. Someday, C.J., you must forgive yourself."

They walked for half an hour, then returned to C.J.'s room. C.J. went inside to see if Ann wanted to talk to Eric, but came out a few minutes later. "She doesn't want to talk to anyone."

When Eric returned to his room an hour later, Janice was asleep, but there was a note pinned to his pillow. It read, "Wake me up when you come in. I love you. Janice."

He sat down beside her and stroked her hair.

"I'm back."

She opened her eyes, sat up, stretched, got up, and padded into the bathroom again.

When she came out, he put his arms around her and they kissed.

There was a knock at the door.

Eric and Janice tiptoed into the bathroom and shut the door.

"Eric," she said softly, "I know the answer to Ann's question about Goldilocks and the Three Bears. The reason Mama Bear's porridge was so cold is that she served it first, then waited for her husband, who was a bishop, to spend some time with her without them being interrupted."

They could still hear the knocking on the door.

Eric sighed. "It's no use." He left Janice in the bathroom and went to answer the door.

It was C.J. again. "Ann decided she wants to talk to you. But not in our room. It's such a mess now. While I was gone, she took my clothes and laid them on the floor so they'd get wrinkled. Can we use your room? I brought the two chairs for the bathroom."

Eric nodded and returned to the bathroom door and knocked.

"Yes, what is it?" Janice asked through the door.

"Ann's coming here," he said.

She opened the bathroom door and angrily breezed past him. "I'm out of the mints," she said abruptly.

"She doesn't want any."

"Eric, I don't like you talking to Ann alone in the middle of the night."

"C.J. asked me if I would. It's an emergency."

"It always is," she muttered.

She slipped her robe on. C.J. came in with the chairs again. Janice got into bed with her magazine. A minute later, Ann rushed in, wearing a white terrycloth robe, looking embarrassed and depressed.

Janice didn't even offer her any cookies.

Eric and Ann went into the bathroom and closed the door.

Ann didn't sit down. She looked at the toiletry items on the counter.

"You have Colgate toothpaste," she said.

"Yes."

"I've always liked the taste, but C.J. always says we can't afford it so I buy a generic brand."

Eric nodded.

Several seconds of silence passed.

"It's called *Toothpaste*," she added.

"Ann, I know you've had a shock tonight. If you want to talk about it . . ."

"Don't expect me to cry," she said numbly. "Do you know what I was doing the night he was with that woman? I was sanding our picnic table. We bought it secondhand and it needed some work, but C.J. was always so busy. So while he was gone, I decided to surprise him. I surprised him—but not as much as he surprised me."

She picked up the Colgate toothpaste and held it, almost lovingly.

"My husband was unfaithful. Unfaithful—it's such an interesting word, isn't it? I think a definition would be disloyal."

"Yes, that's what it means."

"We have our milk delivered," she rambled, "mainly because our milkman is a member of the Church. He has six children, and one boy on a mission. Things are really tight for his family. The dairy he works for makes cottage cheese, but I don't like it. I prefer another brand. Sometimes I sneak to a store and buy the other brand, but I always feel guilty because I think of our milkman and his six children and his son on a mission—and I don't want to be disloyal. So I worry about cottage cheese, and my husband goes on a trip and commits the worst possible act of disloyalty—all the while I'm sanding his picnic table."

"He wasn't thinking."

"Unfaithful," she repeated. "I can't get it to sink in. It's just a word. How can a word be so destructive? Maybe there are other ways of saying it. My husband is in love with another woman. My husband doesn't love me anymore, and maybe he never did. Maybe he's been faking it from the very beginning, from our first night together."

She shuddered.

For the next few minutes she just sat quietly, her head down, her shoulders slumped, her fingers folded neatly together in her lap, her body rocking back and forth slightly. It was the way Eric remembered her mother when she suffered the pain of arthritis.

A tear broke loose and slid down her face.

"I think it's beginning to sink in now," she moaned.

"Ann, I don't think you should torture yourself like this."

She didn't seem to hear him.

"That hurts the worst, to know that he's just been putting up with me, dreaming about other women all the time. I guess my role was to take up where his mother left off—making sure he had clean shirts."

Her fingers ran lightly over her hair as she stared at the floor. "Why did he do it?"

"He wasn't thinking."

More tears ventured forth—apologetic, timid tears, afraid of being seen, tears that ran quietly down her face, to be quickly hidden away again by her terrycloth robe.

But then finally the tears broke loose, coursing in streams down her face. She held onto a single strand of hair and curled the end over and over about her fingers, holding in her other hand the tube of toothpaste.

"He doesn't love me—he never loved me," she repeated again and again to herself, rocking back and forth.

A few minutes later she took a fresh tissue, wiped her face, blew her nose, and said she'd better go.

As she stood up, she still had the toothpaste in her hand.

"Can I borrow it tonight?"

"Sure, you can have it."

"I need something to look forward to," she said.

He walked with her to her room, carrying the chairs.

When they entered the room, C.J. stood up.

He was in bad shape.

"I have to talk to you both," he said.

They sat down. The floor was strewn with his clothes.

"My whole life this past two years has been a lie. And today even when I tried to tell the truth, I still lied. I lied about not knowing her before. I'd met her the year before. We'd written to each other."

"So if you wrote, you know her name," Ann said.

"Her name is Sharon."

"And so you wrote all year, met this one time and committed adultery, and that's all there was to it. Tell me that was the way it was." She sounded as if she desperately wanted it to be that way.

"It wasn't—there was more than one time," he said.

"How many, C.J.?"

"We met six times over the last two years."

"Six times," Ann repeated dully. "You're sure it was six?"

He nodded. "Somehow I always knew it'd come out, and I'd end up having to confess what I'd done, and someone would ask how many times I'd been with her. It's strange that all that can be compacted down to a number. Six times."

"Is she married too?" Ann asked.

"Yes, but she doesn't get along with her husband very well."

"And what did you tell her about me?"

"What does it matter?" C.J. asked.

"There must have been something you said to justify what you were doing."

C.J. stared at the floor and mumbled, "I said you didn't understand me."

"What don't I understand about you, C.J.? Except, of course, for what you've done to our marriage."

He sighed. "I don't know, Ann."

"Just tell me what you told her," she said.

He sighed. "All right, I told her I don't like being your dad's whipping boy. I don't like him telling me how to run the business, even if it is his. I want to be my own man. Ann, I don't like your father, and I don't like working for him."

"You've never said anything to me."

"I didn't want to hurt you," he said.

"Oh, C.J.," she moaned.

"Is Sharon a member of the Church?" Eric asked.

"No, but once I gave her a pamphlet."

"I want to know all about her," Ann said. "How old is she?"

"Twenty-seven."

"Does she have any children?"

"One."

"Where did you meet her when you got together?"

"In a hotel."

"Did you have supper with her sometimes?"

"Sometimes."

"In your room or in the restaurant?"

"What does it matter?"

"I need to know every detail—the color of her eyes, her hair style, what she wore. I hope you paid more attention to her than you do to me. I want to know everything. It's going to eat at me until I know."

"Can't we just forget about it?"

"Forget about it?" she cried out. "I can't forget about it. Why didn't you just say you hated me and get it over with?"

"I never stopped loving you—not really."

Ann ran to a suitcase and pulled out a pair of scissors, ripped open the covers of the bed, pulled out the top sheet, made a cut, then ripped the sheet in two, threw half on the floor, and stomped on it.

"That's what I think of this crummy marriage!" she shouted.

C.J. turned to Eric. "Is this the way things work out when you do it your way?"

She threw a pillow at C.J. "Don't you ever use my Oil of Olay again!"

"Ann, I'm going to confess to the bishop about what I've done."

"No you're not!" she snapped. "You're not going to tell anyone else in the world about it, because if you do, I'm leaving you."

Eric interrupted. "Ann, he needs to talk to the bishop. It's the only way he can ever go completely through the repentance process and be forgiven."

"Then I don't want him forgiven," she said. "I want that ulcer to eat a hole in his stomach! And I'll tell you what else—I don't want other women in the ward talking about Poor Ann—and I don't want to explain why Daddy can't take the sacrament anymore."

She threw a shoe at him. He ducked. It hit the wall.

"Are you going to divorce me?"

"Of course I am! My plans are already made. I'm moving to Utah to find me another husband. There's such a demand for thirty-eighty-year-old women with three kids. Single men love to marry into that. C.J., why didn't you do this after two years of marriage—when I still had a figure?"

"What do you want me to do?" C.J. asked.

"I want you to suffer!"

She ran into the bathroom crying. Neither of them made any effort to stop her.

They sat and waited. Ten minutes passed before she returned.

She appeared composed when she entered. "Did you ever buy her any gifts?" she asked as if she were asking about someone's vacation trip.

"I don't want to talk about it," C.J. said.

"I do—you can't believe the questions I have. I want to know if you bought things for her. And if you did, did she take them home with her? And if she did, didn't her husband wonder where they came from? Tell me—I want to know."

C.J. held his stomach and moaned. "Bishop, make her stop asking questions."

"Six times," Ann went on. "Let me see if I have it straight. You saw her six times. Is that right?"

C.J. nodded.

"Let me guess—a year ago you came home from a

two-day meeting and bought me an automatic dishwasher. I thought that was so sweet of you. Was that two-day meeting one of those six times? Were you feeling guilty after that trip? Is that why I got the dishwasher?"

C.J. was leaning forward in the chair, his arms folded tightly around his stomach. "I'm sorry, I'm so sorry—I'll make it up to you. You'll see."

"How will you do that?" she cried out. "Will you buy me another dishwasher?"

C.J. looked at her. "I don't know—I guess there's nothing I can do, is there?"

She sat down on the bed, her shoulders slumped. "No, I don't think there is. But please try, or I'm leaving and taking the kids. First of all, you have to break it off with Sharon."

"I already have. I haven't talked to her for three months."

"And I don't see how you can travel anymore on business. I don't know if I'll ever trust you again."

"I'll drop out of the senate race and quit traveling."

"Oh, C.J.," she said almost tenderly, "you wanted to be a senator so much—you'd have been a good one, too."

"It doesn't matter now."

"But we need men in office we can trust," she said, then suddenly stopped. "I'm sorry."

"What have I done?" C.J. moaned. "I've become one of the people I used to criticize."

"Why did you quit seeing her?"

C.J. mumbled an answer.

"I can't hear you."

"She said she wanted to leave her husband and for us to get married."

"And what did you say?"

"I said no."

"Why?"

"Because of the children."

"Oh," she said quietly. "Of course—the children."

"And because I had to decide about my life—what direction I wanted to go. If I went with her, it would be without the Church, and I couldn't do that."

"The children and the Church," she said, as if saying the words would somehow make them reasonable to her ears. It didn't.

"What about me?" she shouted. "Why aren't I important to you?"

C.J. went to put his arms around her, but she backed away. "Get away from me!"

Eric had seen her cry before, in high school when her mother made her slow descent into death. One time they had sat in his car and he had held her close and she had cried until his shirt was damp from her tears.

That was long ago.

He watched the tears stream down her face, then fall onto the floor. What fraction of her was there in high school with him? How many cells in that face were the same as the girl he dated so many years ago?

They stood on top of the mountain. It was in the summer, on a mountain trail, much like the first mountain trail they'd climbed together.

"I know this is hard for you," he said. "How can I help?"

"I need someone to talk to."

"You can talk to me."

"I'd like that. You helped me so much when my mother was sick. You were the only thing that kept me going."

"Ann, I've thought about you through the years."

"I've thought about you too."

They looked at each other the way they used to.

"Eric, could you phone me once in a while?"

He smiled. "Sure—that's what friends are for, isn't it?"

"It'll have to be when C.J.'s at work. He might not understand."

Eric's mind clouded over; black clouds filled his mind. He knew he had crossed the line. He didn't know where it was, or how it had come to be, but it was there. The line was not a line of action, but a line of thought that could lead to action. He had crossed it before but had always retreated from its boundary once he realized where he was.

He wasn't sure if any man today could live and not at least consider the possibility of adultery. When he watched TV or went to movies or listened to song lyrics, it was there—as if sex was fulfilling only outside of marriage. And so there was the line, carefully constructed as a defense. And he had just crossed it.

"Ann, we'll never have this conversation. I'll never tell you I want to be a comfort to you, and I'll never phone you. You'll need help to get through what lies ahead, but I can't help you."

"We'd never go wrong," she said. "I just need a friend."

"I'm a bishop. I've held bishop's courts. I look at men who've committed adultery. They're basically good men, men who love their families, who take an interest in their boys' Little League games and take their families on long vacations, and go into debt to provide their families with a decent Christmas. Men like me, not much difference between us really—except they overrated their ability to resist temptation. They formed friendships with women other than their wives. They figured they were above simple rules, then found out they were not. Janice is my wife, and I'll never betray her. That's why I can't talk to you like I am now."

"You aren't talking to me," she said, fading away. "You're talking with yourself, Eric, not with me."

She faded away, and he was left alone on the mountain with only his thoughts.

* * * * *

A torturous hour passed during which Ann alternated between silent brooding followed by demanding that C.J. tell her some intimate details about his time with Sharon.

Sometimes she just cried.

"I guess you've lost all respect for me now, haven't you," C.J. said.

"Yes, I guess I have," she answered quietly.

Ann sat, a replica of her mother when she suffered

with arthritis, rocking slightly back and forth, her fingers folded neatly on her lap.

Night sounds flickered through the silence. A couple next door argued about his drinking. The argument ended when he left, slamming the door. An unidentified man walked down the hall whistling the school song. In the room next door a TV carried an old war movie. Only the bass sounds penetrated the walls.

From out of that dreary silence came Ann's voice, barely whispering the words from a hymn.

"I know that my Redeemer lives."

Her voice, small and tiny, was nearly swallowed up by the lurking nightmares of the night, but she continued.

"What comfort this sweet sentence gives.
He lives, he lives, who once was dead.
He lives, my ever living head."

C.J. moaned. "Oh, my God, Father in heaven, what have I done?"

Ann's voice grew more hopeful. She sang the chorus.

"He lives to bless me with his love.
He lives to plead for me above.
He lives my hungry soul to feed.
He lives to bless in time of need."

"C.J.?" Ann said quietly.

"Yes?"

"Please hold me."

They sat on the bed, their arms entwined around each other, both of them sobbing. Over and over he told her he was sorry, and she told him again and again she knew he was.

"I'd better go now," Eric said.

"I've confessed everything, bishop," C.J. said. "I'm not much of a man, but at least now I'm honest."

They walked Eric to the door. Ann remembered his toothpaste and gave it back.

"I won't need it. C.J. and I have our own toothpaste."

Eric nodded and left.

A minute later he stood outside his room and realized

he'd left his keys in the room. He knocked, but there was no answer. He knocked louder and called for Janice, but she was asleep. He banged on the door. Somebody next door yelled for him to be quiet.

He looked at his watch. It was three-thirty. He went downstairs to the lounge and sat on a couch and stared one more time at the mountain.

He stood on the mountain once more with Barbara Walters. She gave him a sincere look and asked, "Eric, how does it feel to be nearly forty and still mowing lawns in your neighborhood and running an orange juice stand?"

"Humble, Barbara, humble—but we don't mow. We just fertilize and spray."

"Is it true that for the most part you've been a failure in your life?"

He cleared his throat. "Not everything's worked out the way I thought it would."

"Eric, that's what failure means. And that's why I wanted to talk to you, just the two of us." She looked into the camera. "Because in the past, I've talked to some of the biggest successes in America—men like Reggie Jackson and Paul Newman. Now I wanted to talk to a failure. With your Ph.D. in physics, ending up fertilizing lawns, you're a classic."

"I'm not a failure," he objected. "You haven't said anything about my being a bishop. It takes thirty to forty hours a week, and I do it with no pay as a service to my church."

"So you justify your vocational failure because of your church service—is that right?"

"No, but you have to have priorities."

"I have priorities, Eric. That's why I'm a success. You're the one who needs better priorities. But let's not argue. Do you feel bad tonight?"

"Very bad, Barbara."

Barbara looked into the camera. "Here's a man at the bottom—someone who spent eight years in college and ends up mowing lawns and selling orange juice."

"We don't mow," he mumbled.

"A man who tries to rationalize away his failure with church

service. A man who claims to be religious, yet who tonight considered taking up with his high school girl friend, who's already married."

"Wait a minute—that's not true."

"You're saying you didn't think about calling her once in a while when her husband was at work?"

"But I didn't and I won't—not ever."

"Okay, okay. Let me continue. A man who's considered a joke at his high school reunion. This has got to be your darkest hour—and I want to say, Eric, on behalf of the American people, thanks for letting us share it with you."

She was enjoying this. "How many Eric Turners are out there? We're told there were over two hundred thousand Ph.D.s turned out in the sixties who now work at jobs other than what they were trained for. It's a national tragedy."

The director, off camera, was nodding his head enthusiastically and holding up a sign on a chalkboard that read "More emotion."

"How will history judge Eric Turner? An incompetent? A fool? A religious fanatic?"

Eric had had enough. "Wait a minute—whatever history says about me doesn't matter. What matters is what I say about me. If I feel I've done my best, that's what matters. I'm not a failure. I have a wonderful wife who still loves me, and some terrific kids, and we have our faith in God. I have the priesthood, and I've seen miracles. I won't let you or anyone else tell me I'm a failure."

"A hundred years from now, outside your family, who will know or even care that you lived? Just admit you're a failure and we'll end the interview."

"No, I won't."

"Eric, if you just admit you're a failure, it'll mean success for you. You'll be able to sell the rights to your story. C'mon, just admit it."

"But I'm not a failure."

She shook her head. "You're not even a success at failure, are you? What have you ever done in your life? How many years were you in school? And for what purpose? To fertilize lawns."

"I'm good at what I do. People recommend me to their friends for their lawns. And we have a nice home and I have my priesthood and my temple marriage and faith in the Savior. All in all, that's not too bad for one life, is it? I'm a successful businessman. And my expertise is change. I can change. I can move from square zero to square one. How much do you think I knew about running a business when I started? Nothing. I didn't know anything. But I learned. That's what my education has prepared me for. It's prepared me to accept change. That's what I do best."

"You'll have to change without ABC," Barbara said, packing up her microphone.

"All right then," he said, smiling. "It doesn't matter. I'll keep making changes in my life—not for you—not for history—but for me. Watch me change, Barbara."

But she left him.

He hurried to the laundry room to use the dollar changer, then rushed to the candy machine and bought himself ten dollars' worth of gum.

CHAPTER NINE

It was finished. He looked at his watch—it was five-thirty.

He lay down on the couch and fell asleep.

The next thing he remembered was the cleaning lady standing over him.

"Why do you people always make such a mess of everything?"

He sat up.

A large pile of gum wrappers lay strewn around him.

She picked up the sculpture from the coffee table.

"Careful," he warned, "it's very delicate."

"What is it?"

"A mountain goat. Notice the horns on its head."

"What's it made out of?"

"Chewing gum. It's all I could find last night when I got in the mood to create."

She examined it more carefully. "Well, you're the best gum sculptor we've ever had here, and we get a lot of strange people. Last summer we had a guy who did chain-saw sculptures. He did my face with his chain saw."

"When I was a little boy," Eric said enthusiastically, "I did a mountain goat out of balsa wood, but since then I've never really developed my talent. I've decided to take a night class. And someday I want to do a full-scale statue of my wife."

She whistled in astonishment. "That'll keep you busy chewing, won't it?"

"Probably out of wood or bronze or granite."

"Oh, sure."

"There's another thing you should know about me. I'm a Mormon."

"G'wan, you're no Mormon."

"Why do you say that?"

"Well, you seem so nice . . . I mean, I guess I haven't known any Mormons before. I've accepted Christ as my personal Savior."

"Good for you. So have I."

"Really? I didn't think Mormons were Christians."

"Sure we are."

"And you say you've accepted the Lord into your life?"

"Oh, yes."

"And you're going to be saved in heaven?"

"To tell you the truth, it's a little early to say yet."

"You don't know?"

"It depends on how I live the rest of my life."

"But the Bible says you're saved by the grace of the Lord."

"Yes, but the Book of Mormon clarifies it. We're saved by grace after all we can do. We have to live the commandments as best as we can. Do you have a Bible?"

"Sure do. Look, while we talk, could you help me clean up around here? If I don't have this place clean by seven, I'm in real trouble."

They worked and talked together.

"I guess we don't agree," he finally said after the room was clean.

"I guess not."

"Say, would you come to a church service here this morning? We'll be telling people about what we believe."

"I have my own church," she said.

"Sure. At least take a pamphlet from the mantel, okay?"

She grabbed a pamphlet, then went upstairs with him and unlocked his door. Janice was still asleep.

He woke her up to look at his gum sculpture.

"It's very nice," she said sleepily.

A minute later he crawled into bed.

"Eric, why were you talking to C.J. and Ann last night?"

"I can't tell you."

"You're not their bishop. You shouldn't have to talk to them. You've been as busy with other people's problems up here as you are back home."

"Janice, I'm very tired."

"I don't want you talking to Ann alone. Do you still care for her?"

"You're the only woman I care about that way. Janice, please, I've got to sleep now."

"What about the meeting this morning?"

"Forget it. Nobody will come. There's nobody in the class of '61 who wants to know about the Church."

"Eric, I want to talk about my life. That woman at the softball game got me thinking. I've made a decision."

"What?" he said sleepily.

"I want to be me."

"You *are* you, Janice."

"No, that's not me. It's somebody else. Now I want to be me."

"Who are you?"

"That woman yesterday said I could be a leader of our nation."

He gave a long, frustrated, sleepy sigh.

"I need outside interests now that the children are in school. You know, I have a trained singing voice. I'm tired of singing only for weddings and funerals. In the first place, the people getting married don't care about the songs. They just want to get it over with. And I've sung at so many funerals that people see me in the hall at church and start crying as a reflex action. Eric, in March of this year, the civic theater group is putting on *H.M.S. Pinafore*, and I want to try out for the part of Josephine, the female romantic lead. If I wait any longer in my life, I'll only be good for the part of Buttercup, poor little

Buttercup. I need to use my talents. Does that make sense to you?"

Eric started to snore.

She listened to the noises coming from his mouth. "Somehow I always knew it would come to this," she said to nobody in particular.

* * * * *

Three hours later there was a knock at the door. Eric opened his eyes and looked at his watch. He struggled out of bed and opened the door. It was Ryan.

"Bishop, we're waiting for you."

"What for?"

"Our meeting."

"Is there anyone there besides Michelle and C.J. and Ann?"

"About twenty others."

"You're kidding."

Ten minutes later Eric and Janice walked into the lodge room.

Eric sat on the stand with Ryan, while Janice sat in the front row. Two men sitting near Janice were looking at a pamphlet.

"I could join the Mormons if it weren't for this," one said to the other, pointing to something in the pamphlet.

"I don't see why that's a problem for you," the other said. "Look over here, it's quoting the Bible, and it says . . ."

Good grief, Eric thought, they're converting each other.

C.J. and Ann stood in the hall. They motioned to Eric to come and talk to them.

"Can I come to your meeting?" C.J. asked. "If you don't want me, I'll stay in the hall and listen."

"And I'll stay with him," Ann said.

Eric put his arm around C.J.'s shoulder and hugged him. "You come in with us."

"Eric," Ann said, "we've decided to do it the right way. I'll go with C.J. when he goes to talk to the bishop. If there's a court, I'll go with him to that. Whatever happens, we want to stick together through it all." She paused, then added, "if we can."

"It'll work out for you both. C.J., will you give the closing prayer for our meeting?"

"I'm not worthy."

"You're more worthy now than you've been for two years. It'll be an honor for us to hear you pray."

They sang "Onward, Christian Soldiers" for their opening hymn, with Janice leading the singing. Then Michelle gave the opening prayer.

Ryan talked about the restoration of the gospel.

As Ryan spoke, Eric found himself looking at Janice. It was a face he loved, a face that over the years had carried every emotion. He gloried in her beauty and grace and delicate symmetry. There were a few gray hairs and small lines on her face. In coming years, whether or not she put mashed avocado on it, the lines would become furrows.

They were getting older.

He loved her—now more than ever before.

Sometimes late at night after spending time with other people's problems, he would go home and just hold her close. He couldn't tell her what he heard in counseling, and she never asked. They'd turn off the lights in the living room and hold each other and watch the shadows move on the wall as the cars turned the corner near the house. He would hold her and tell her over and over how much he loved her, how much he needed her, that without her he couldn't go on as a bishop. That would always surprise her, and she'd ask, "What do I do?"

"You're my best friend. I can count on you."

Sometimes she'd kiss him and whisper softly, "Let the

ward members sustain you in their way—I'll sustain you in mine."

She was available for him, and that certainty was a blessing—that he could go to her and express his needs and have her respond, and that she could come to him with hers. They never had gone anywhere else but to each other.

He looked again at the tiny lines around her eyes. A million smiles and worries—they were the evidence of their life together. She was his best part. So much of the time he felt overwhelmed, a quivering mass of No and Never and Impossible. But she believed in him, and he trusted in her good judgment.

Ryan finished his talk, and Michelle spoke about the family. Then it was Eric's turn.

"Do you have any questions?" he asked.

Jerry, the M.C. of the program the night before, stood up. "This pamphlet says you have a prophet, just like Moses, and that God talks to him. Is that really true?"

"Yes, it is."

"And you believe it?"

"I do."

"Okay, if it's true, then that's pretty big news, isn't it? Eric, I've known you since we were in grade school, and you've never said anything to me about this. Why didn't you tell us—if it's true and important to you."

Eric sighed. "I've always waited for the perfect moment to talk about my beliefs, and then later in my life I waited for me to be perfect. You know, that's never going to happen. I've waited too long. Let me change that now. There is a prophet on the earth today. Jesus does speak to us today through prophets and apostles. And from now on I'm not waiting to tell people about it."

C.J. gave the closing prayer. They had people sign up if they wanted to know more about the Church. Eleven people signed up. Two of the eleven were Martha Wilson and her husband.

"I knew we'd do it!" Michelle burst out as they shook hands.

They had breakfast together, then walked in the garden and looked at the flowers. There were some bees on some of the flowers, and Eric told about their ward welfare project and about queen bees.

"During the summer a queen bee will lay an egg every fifteen seconds. She has to do that, because a worker bee in the summer only lasts for three weeks. It literally works itself to death."

"How long does a queen bee last?" Michelle asked.

"About three years. You can tell when you have to change her. When she's young, she lays the eggs in nice regular patterns, one after the other, in the brood chamber. But an old queen bee will lay erratically, laying one here and then another one on the other side of the frame. That's when you have to get a new queen bee for the good of the hive."

Ann and Janice stayed together in the garden while C.J. paid his bill and Ryan put their suitcase in the car. Eric phoned his first counselor at church.

"Bishop, something's up. President Baxter wants to set up interviews next week with all the Melchizedek Priesthood in the ward, and he keeps asking when you'll be back."

Suddenly Eric knew what was happening.

He phoned President Baxter at the stake office.

"President, are you about to release me as bishop?"

There was a long silence on the other end. Then President Baxter nervously cleared his throat. "I'd like to have a chance to talk to you and your wife."

"I know."

"It's been four years, bishop."

"I understand. When the queen bee gets tired, you have to make a change."

"What?"

"I'll tell you about it later."

"I wish you could be here with me so we could talk. You've done an excellent job."

"So I am going to be released?" Eric asked.

"Well . . . yes, you are."

Eric was stunned. He ended the conversation and quickly walked outside and onto the trail he had hiked the day before.

It was over.

"So they don't even want you as a bishop, do they," Barbara said.

"I guess not."

"You're very depressed now, aren't you."

"Yes, I am."

"Why? Being released will give you forty extra hours a week. Why aren't you happy about it?"

"You wouldn't understand."

She touched his sleeve. "Maybe I will. Trust me."

"When I was a bishop, God answered my prayers."

"And now God won't answer your prayers?"

He looked at her.

"I guess he will—not about the ward, but just about my own life."

She shook her head. "What do you mean—just about your own life? I know about your life—that alone'll keep God busy. You people are all a little strange, aren't you?"

"We're a peculiar people, Barb."

"Yes you are, and don't ever call me Barb again." She left.

On top of a ridge, he made his way to a large outcropping of rock where he knelt down and prayed. He mourned for the imminent loss of the mantle of a bishop. He felt like a banana peel—used and tossed away.

It was the Savior who made it worthwhile to be a bishop. Bishops come to feel the kind of unconditional love that Jesus has for every individual. There were those who had made serious mistakes, who were beyond what anyone would consider worth salvaging, their lives in shambles, no goals, no self-worth, no hope. Yet when

Eric talked with them, he felt Jesus' love, His unwillingness to give up or to write them off. With the Savior there were no disposables, no throw-away lives.

That made it worthwhile, made it worth the time and stress and late nights in his office at church. Jesus worked with bishops. And now Eric would no longer be a bishop.

He pleaded in his prayer for some calling in the Church that in some way would make up for that loss. But he suspected that nothing would ever measure up.

He returned to the room. Janice was putting things in the suitcase.

"They're going to release me," he said painfully.

"How do you know?"

"I just talked to President Baxter. If I could've done a little better, maybe he wouldn't be releasing me."

"Don't say that—you were the best bishop in the world."

She put her arms around him and kissed him. He let himself be cradled in her arms.

"Eric, I have a little confession to make," she said a few minutes later.

"What?"

"I've been praying for you to be released as a bishop."

"Why?"

"I couldn't see how I was going to manage with another baby without you at home to help."

"But you've never complained."

"You had enough problems to deal with. I'll tell you the night I started to pray for your release from being a bishop. It was a few weeks ago, after the Pine Wood Derby at Cub Scouts. Do you remember? All the other fathers worked with their sons to carve the cars and paint 'em. But you came home the same day of the race, and, between phone calls, knocked out something for Brent. His was the only car there with wet paint. I remember it left a little paint trail down the slope. It came in last. Brent was so embarrassed about it. He cried that night and asked why Dad never helped him in Cub Scouts. I told him you were busy and he asked, 'Too busy for me?' "

"I never knew," Eric said. "He cried about it?"

"That night he did. Some boy had told him his car looked like cow manure."

"Cow manure?"

"Yes."

"The color or the design?"

"He didn't say."

Eric sat down on the bed. "Cow manure."

She sat down beside him.

"I love you very much, Eric."

"And I love you. I'm sorry if I haven't been the kind of husband I should have been. It seems like for the last four years, I was always hurrying out the door. Well, things will be different now. I promise I'll be a full-time husband and father. I'll change diapers, even the messy ones."

She gave him a quick hug.

"Eric, when do we have to check out?"

"Two o'clock, why?"

"We really haven't gotten our money's worth out of the room yet, have we?"

A slight smile flashed across his face. "No, we really haven't."

A minute later they were both brushing their teeth in the bathroom.

She looked in the mirror. "I can't believe it. Just because this is a high school reunion, I'm getting a pimple."

"It's all those cookies and mints you've been eating."

"Since we were in high school, they've found out chocolate and fried foods don't cause acne after all."

Eric frowned. "Now they tell us."

They sat in bed and talked and held hands. He folded his legs under him.

"I want to be in a musical this spring," she said. "The

theater group is putting on *H.M.S. Pinafore*. I want to try out for it."

"I'll stay home and watch the kids for you during practices. I owe you four years of that."

There was a knock at the door. They kept very quiet.

The doorknob turned. Eric remembered he hadn't locked it after the cleaning lady let him in. Janice dove under the covers. Eric grabbed the skiing magazine and pretended to be reading.

Ace and Bunny opened the door and looked at them sitting in bed.

"Hey, what's happening, cousin?" Ace boomed out. "We were heading this way, so we thought, hey, we're family now, why don't we just drop by and say hello on our way to the California beaches."

"I love the slacks," Bunny said.

"Would you like a cookie?" Janice said automatically.

Eric leaned over and whispered to her. "You don't have to do that anymore."

"I don't? I don't have to be gracious?"

He shook his head. "Not all the time. It's one of the advantages of having a husband who's not a bishop anymore."

She grinned. "Hey you two! Bug off! Can't you see we're busy now?"

Bunny smiled. "Like she says, they're busy. C'mon, Ace, we'd better go."

Ace laughed. "He looks just like Kuan Yin, doesn't he, with his legs folded like that."

"Just like him," Bunny agreed.

"Who's Kuan Yin?" Eric asked.

"A seventeenth century Chinese sculptor. Kuan Yin was an enlightened person who helped others. With your legs folded that way, you look like him. Well, see you around."

"Wait a minute," Eric called out. "How do you know about a seventeenth century sculptor?"

"I have a Ph.D. in art history. Got it in '74 but couldn't get a job. So I just climbed on my bike and I've been going ever since."

"No kidding! I have a Ph.D. too, and I couldn't get a job either, so now I do lawns and have an Orange Julius stand." Eric started laughing, then Janice joined in, then Ace and Bunny.

Eric showed Ace his gum sculpture. Ace said it showed promise.

"Do you ever work?" Eric asked.

"Not much, not since graduate school. I worked then."

"Sure. Look, I'm going to need some time to myself to learn about sculpturing. If you wanted to, maybe you could come and work for me in my business. If you'll wait an hour for us, we'll talk about it."

Ace turned to Bunny with a grin. "I'm gonna be Lawn Intern!"

"Oh," Janice added, "there're some pamphlets on the fireplace mantel. It's about our church—if you want to read 'em while you wait."

Ace hugged Bunny. "Wouldn't it be a kick if we became Mormons and I ended up mowing lawns?"

They left laughing.

"Missionary work," Eric said. "That's what I want to do now."

Eric locked the door and turned to face Janice with a wide grin. "Everything's going to turn out all right. I don't feel bad anymore. In fact, I feel like doing something wild and crazy!"

"Like what?" she asked, sounding a little worried.

"Like eating cookies in bed and not giving a hang about the crumbs!"

And that's what they did.

* * * * *

A long stretch of highway, a lone gas station run by an old man, Pop Miller.

A motorcycle pulls up to the pump. A man takes off his helmet and starts pumping gas.

His female companion saunters into the restroom.

Pop Miller always gets a little worried with motorcyclists. You never know these days. He hovers near the pump keeping an eye on things, making sure they don't run off without paying.

"I got a question for you," the man says.

"What?" Pop says, sounding worried.

"How much do you know about the Mormon Church?"

A minute later the man and the woman, who is very much pregnant, leave.

Pop Miller looks curiously at the pamphlets they left him and asks himself—Who was that helmeted man and his faithful woman companion?

* * * * *

"You think Ace and Bunny'll beat us back in our car?" Janice yells above the roar of the cycle.

Eric laughs. "Are you kidding? In our car?"

They lustily sing the song she's taught him earlier that day, a song from the musical *H.M.S. Pinafore*:

We sail the Ocean blue
And our saucy ship's a beauty;
We're sober folks and true,
And attentive to our duty.
When the balls whistle free
O'er the bright blue sea,
We stand to our guns all day;
When at anchor we ride

At the Portsmouth tide,
We've plenty of time for play!
Ahoy! Ahoy!
We've plenty of time for play!

Eric looks down the long stretch of open highway and opens the cycle up a little more.